Robert Williams Jr. (ARTHUR)

"Axel And Daniel, First Love Journey"

(Book Series 1Of 3)

TABLE OF CONTENT:

(No More Hiding) Daniel and I decided to live as a same sex couple. I'm sorry for not talking to you first...

(Chapter) VI

(We Are Family) Axel asked, are you ready? Jamal answered, I am, and I have condoms too...

Publish by Kindle/direct publishing.

Published 2022. This erotic, gay fiction is intended for all adults, 18 years old and above.

Printed in the United States of America

ISBN: 9798848510560

ASIN: BOB82QTFZN, Author's contact, rwilliams.williams74@gmail.com, rwilliams.williams@att.net

"Mom I'm gay. I grappled with the thought in my mind before I came to this conclusion, it's clear to me, It feels normal to Daniel and I. For me I was like a dragon flower waiting to bloom; I was not coerced, guided, or taking advantage of. Daniel and I decided"

AXEL AND DANIEL, LOVE JOURNEY

Robert Williams Jr,

Author

"The First"

Chapter I

I grew up in Dallas Texas; My name is Axel Kingston Junior I am 18 years old, bilingual young man, growing and changing rapidly. I didn't' understand at the time what made me different, I just knew based on my transformation and how I felt and my interest. Raymond, my brother, treated me like someone he always needed to protect. My dad, Mr. Kingston spent much of his time drinking and he fought with my mother, consistently. (That's the part of growing up I am not too proud of.)

My dad was not pleased with how things turned out for him as a father and husband, he had a tough time finding a job, he worked small, odd jobs but nothing permanent. He stayed home most of the time hanging out with our neighbors drinking all day; my mother went to school to get her GED, and her master's degree, she has a career in engineering, working for a company called Electronic Instruments of Texas, she became management of the PC Board Designing Department. She saved her money, planned to buy a home, she's in a government assist program that helps her with our housing and our education, she worked to get me in one of the best schools in Texas.

However, I must say my dad was genuinely warmhearted to me, he would say regularly, "You're my special son," I loved him, to me he is the best father anyone could have, I felt safer with him around. We had some good times but, my dad drinking situation progressed, that's when it became a problem for the family.

My family accepted me for who I am although, he and my mom were aware of my dilemma; My mom did not openly express her feelings, but she treated me like I was special in a way different from Raymond; She kept a close watch on me.

Most of the time Raymond and I were together, that's how I was able to meet his friends they were all older guys; I had my own friends, but they were not mature enough for me I would always be bored, and is seemed I had different interest, we were not on the same level. (Not to mention, our place was too small to have friends over, we could have one or maybe two friends at a time, and we could not entertain guest in our bedrooms.)

Raymond's friend, Michael, he was our neighbor, he lived three units away from us. One day I noticed Michael looking at me in a very peculiar way, which made me curious, I also noticed him looking at my dick on the low; Once, we were all together I walked off and suddenly turned around and caught Michael looking at my ass, he smiled at me, I felt a vibe that sparked my interest.

Raymond has a hard-boiled personality, there's nothing about Raymond that says gay, my brother is to me obnoxious, but I love him, he's my first friend; I cannot see how Michael and he were friends. I later understood my brother better, He didn't have a problem with queer guys, he felt people should be able to love who they love, but during that time he never talk to me about sex.

The first time I ever been with a guy Raymond's age alone in a bedroom, was with Michael. He invited me to go with him to his mother's apartment, I accepted his invite, we were alone at his mom's house I was curious to know why, I wasn't sure.

The realization came to me, I was about to have my first homosexual experience; Michael asked me to follow him upstairs to his room and said, Axel you can get comfortable, no one is home, do you want to lie in bed with me? I laid in bed next to him, when he asked me to lie in bed with him I thought why he is so sure I could be interested in doing something like this, but I did, curious to what might happen next; he turned over toward me and kissed me on my cheek, then he pulled his pants down I was totally surprised; he was not wearing underwear he had a boner; he is twenty-one years old. Michael kissed me touching me in ways that was not familiar to me, I had never been touch in that way before, intentionally. He guided my hand to his hard dick and said you like it? I didn't answer him; I wasn't very comfortable. (Which added more confusion, but it was a fascinating experience to see a hard dick other than Raymond and mine.) There wasn't much more happened after that, I didn't take my clothes off because I wasn't sure what to do, he wasn't doing much talking I was confused to how we should get started, I had a boner, ready to do whatever he wanted to do but he needed to take the lead.

I told him I must go; I thought to myself, this isn't the right person or time, I left going home but this opened my mind to more curiosity.

That did not happen anymore until after we moved. We stayed in the neighborhood for a year after that experience and during that time I was just a young impressionable guy, growing with many questions, processing the short homosexual experience I encountered. I avoided Michael, so he never got a chance to explain to me what happened between us, I struggled processing it; I was on my own. I thought about him often, when I did, I would get an erection, I still did not know much about sex or same-sex attraction; however, this is when I first came to the knowledge of my sexuality or my sexual interest. It was very confusing because I still didn't know where it came from. in fact, it felt normal. What was not so ordinary for me is I look so different from everyone.

My mom explained to me at an early age why my dad and I look so different; "she said you and your dad has a rare blood disorder called vitiligo, which caused your skin, hair, and eyes to change color. Axel asked, will we continue changing? No, your doctor doesn't expect you will, am I a healthy person? Yes Axel, you're as healthy as your dad, you don't need to worry; you are growing up as well as expected. My parents taught me not to think of myself as different because I look different from others, "you are the same as I am and everyone else."

(Let's go back to my upbringing).

My family and I went to church, we always had dinner together, we were Christians, I don't think during that time my parents really knew what that meant. My dad side of the family were erudite people, religious and judgmental people but loving and caring. My cousins occasionally expressed I have same sex interests because, I didn't drool over the girls, but Raymond would control the narrative.

My mom shared with us minimum of her history and her side of the family, her family was small, I knew my grandmother but outside of her I did not really know anyone. My mother said she was a noticeably young girl, she left home at an early age; 12 years old, her mother did not want her around her stepfather, she did not trust him she sent my mother to Texas to live with her older cousin, which was not much older, said by many her cousin was a bad influence. My mom wasn't happy with how things turned out for her as a kid, she said she missed things kids does, was unhappy about not getting an education so she was adamant that her son receives a good education; during the summers my parents sent Raymond and I to study Spanish and French, education is very important to her, she said we'll need to speak more than the English language to communicate with other ethnicities.

During this time, my mom met my dad, she was just a kid, was pregnant with Raymond. My mother had a brother that joined the Army Branch at age 18, and a half-brother that lived in California by my mother's biological father. Her brother married while in the army to my dad's sister, he helped my mom by sending her money while in the Military; My mother's cousins were unknown to us; my mother was sixteen when she had her first child illegitimate, which is my half-brother, Raymond. Therefore, I am my dad's only biological son; Hindsight I did see my father showing favoritism toward me, it was probably because of our skin condition.

Consequently, there weren't anything abnormal in my upbringing, my parents are liberals and open-minded people, that's how my brother and I was raised. My dad wasn't faithful to my mom, she never said but it was obvious, that's the impression my dad left with me, it's possible I'll have that trait later in life. Once My father embarrassed me, he expressed that I were different; playfully he was hitting me in the chest, saying "I am going to make a man out of you." I have never seen or heard my father expressed that I were different until then;

Nevertheless, I loved him, we were close. Thereafter, my dad said let's take a ride and wash the car, we will go to the park afterwards to hang out. We went to the carwash, washed the car and then we left to go to the park, but my dad took a detour to the liquor store; We never made it to the park, instead we went to a strange lady's house. The only time I saw her was when she opened the door and yelled out, hello Axel Junior! Waving to me, I was surprised she knew my name, I yelled back to her, hello ma'am! My father yelled, "Axel Junior stay in the car; wait for me." As if I had a choice.

I waited for what seemed like forever. Finally, he came out staggering from side to side attempted to lose his balance, he got into the car to drive us home, I asked, should I drive dad? The question was rhetorical, I really don't know how to drive; He replied, maybe next time; he ran through red lights, driving onto the curb all the way home in my mom's new car; I was afraid, but I didn't want to express it because I wanted to show how brave I am. My dad made a point for me to understand I have to be a stand-up, take-charge kind of person. "He said you're going to be a very important person." It would have been more informative if he talked to me about my sexuality, so I could have had some knowledge about sex, No one talked to me about it because they weren't sure about what type I would be interested in.

We made it home and when we did my mother asked him with a loud tone, "where did you go with my son"? He explained, but no one could understand him because when he spoke his words slurred, sounded like nonsense, he and my mother fought until bedtime which was very frightening. However, being with my father was love to me, my dad wanted me to hang out with him, that was perfect for me.

We finally moved to the other side of town, University Park, north Side of Dallas, Texas, upper class, multiracial neighborhood. We all were excited my mom and dad seemed incredibly happy. They were first time home buyers, the house is a four bedroom, living room, family room, office, two car garage, large front, and back lawn, also with a large chef kitchen. (We had never been in a home so large).

However, their marriage took a turn for the worse, my dad could not control his drinking, he was out of control; my mother told him to move out she did not want him around us in that condition, she said to him, "you need to get some help;"

the next day he was gone we did not see him for years; my mother, Raymond and I was glum but later cheered up, we all had infinite shared love for him. Later my mom decided to get a divorced, she said, "I divorced dad, it just wasn't working for us."

My mom is now a single Parent, with an excellent career that covers her mortgage and household expenses, she kept the new car, my dad did not take anything with him other than his clothes and small items. I wasn't sure if I would ever see my dad again, but in my heart, I felt he will come back because I knew he loved me, I'm his special son, he said.

My mother, during the summer transferred me to my new High School; I'm in the 12th grade, but I have already started taking college freshman courses, because I completed all of my high school courses sooner than expected, I'm a fast learner. My life has significantly changed, I embraced my sexual interests, the ideal of living a homosexual lifestyle, my same sex attraction became clearer to me, it wasn't something I could overlook.

The first person I met in our new neighborhood were a tall guy with an excellent body physique, it's the first thing I noticed; I became interested with excitement running through my mind. I were wearing shorts with a tight fit t-shirt, lounging around the house reading, I weren't expecting to meet anyone, I knew I would get a boner if he approached me, because my dick stayed hard often, it didn't take much for me to get a boner.

He came from three houses from us, on the street where we just moved to; I saw him walking toward me at a fast pace, I was on the porch admiring the new neighborhood, he stopped in front of our home and said to me, hello my name is Daniel, he asked do you speak

Spanish? I replied, Si co'mo esta's. Daniel respondo, estoy genial!

He went on asking, where did you all move from? I said, we moved from West Dallas. Instantaneously, Daniel said to me, "you are gay," I replied, really, what gave you that idea? He said, because you are an unusually pretty guy with noticeable blue eyes; your shorts are tight, and you have a big dick print, what's up with that? I looked down at myself and said that's because I have to pee. He laughed and said, I thought it was because you liked my strong physique, I'm a football quarterback, damn, I wanted you to like my body, do you think I have a good-looking bod? I answered, do you really need my opinion; so that's why you think I'm gay? Daniel said, there's more to it, I'll explain it to you later. He then laughed again, then he asked, "do you like guys,"? I answered innocently, yes. (We weren't on the same page).

He went on to asked, "have you ever kissed the guy," (I answered yes, I was thinking about Michael and me), and then he looked at me with wide opened eyes staring deep into my big light blue eyes, practically drooling, "he asked do you want to kiss me?" I said no. Then he asked me for my phone number, he happen to have an ink pen in his pocket, (go figure). He wrote my number on his arm, said I will call you, do not tell anyone about what we talked about it is our secret, it's not that it's something wrong with our conversation, it's just that you will need more informaci'on.

I asked, Daniel are you gay, have you been with a guy before? He said, fuck no dude, I just know things.

Finally, he asked what is your name? I answered, Axel Kingston Junior. He laughed again, he asked jokingly, what should I call you, big boner Junior? I said, no, you can call me Mr. Kingston. He said, okay Junior, walking away laughing, and said Bye Axel, still laughing, he said you better go take care of that pee situation, your dick is huge, I said thanks dude, I'm glad you noticed; I was very surprised by how he openly came on to me. Then he said he's not gay, I thought, what the fuck. I knew I was extremely interested; my body was responding, I got a boner while he was talking to me, especially when he was admiring my dick on the low.

Frequently, Daniel and I talked over the phone it wasn't easy for me to talk over the phone because my mom and brother tends to be overprotective. Therefore, I were limited to what I could say to him over the phone, we didn't hang out together until later, when we became closer, we only talked over the phone.

He did ask me all the right questions, like anyone, he asked me about my unusually, what he called attractiveness, I said, I'm glad you asked, so we can get this out of the way. I said, Daniel I'm an African American, my attractiveness is called, Vitiligo; which started when I was a baby, it changed my appearance gradually made everything turn whitish, my entire body, the good thing is it isn't contagious; I asked is it a deal breaker for you, we can't be friends now? He replied, on the contrary, you are going to be my best friend. I respond, Great, so you think I'm a cool and interesting person? Daniel answered, yes and sexy too.

I felt lustful and wanted him to ask me for sex; but I waited because I did not know where to start, and I wasn't sure about approaching him in that way; (sabia que e'l queria mierda). I knew he wanted me.

One late night he called it was during a weekend, my mom allowed us to stay up late on weekends. Raymond answered the phone, he called me to the phone and said, "es un tipo, dijo que su nombre es Daniel." I said thanks dude, now give me the fucking phone dude and get out so I can talk in peace.

I said hello, Daniel said axel the night is the night, I said for what? He said come to my house I'll meet you at the back door I am home alone, I asked where is your mother and dad? He said they're at work late tonight, my mother working nights this weekend; I went on to asked, what about your brother? He's staying at our cousin's house this weekend.

(Daniel only has one sibling, Paul, twenty-two years old, I must admit he is very sexy.)

I anxiously headed toward his home with the hopes we will do what Michael and I did and more because I wanted to experience releasing my buildup in him. We talked about the fact that I had never experienced an orgasm. (Sometimes I would wake up in the mornings with wet, sticky underwear, but it wasn't from something I acknowledged as pleasurable.)

That excited him he looked forward to assist, he promised to go easy because it could be a little painful the first time. I really did not know what to expect, I have never had sex and never masturbated, (He assured me he will figure things out).

I arrived, he said come in, are you afraid? I answered, no, should I be? He pulled me into his arms and kissed me with his mouth wide opened and his tongue deep inside of my mouth, shagging my arse, I pushed away from him and said, hold on dude, he pulled me back into his arms and said, you are okay I got you; I want hurt you, you can relax.

I asked, what are we going to do? He said let's go to my room and take your clothes off. I followed him, he was already undressed, only wearing his boxer shorts, I started by removing my shirt and from there he takes over, in total control, my boner stood out like a poll. We laid back on his bed and he begins by licking my pezones, he went down with his tongue to my dick, pleasuring my hard boner two minutes later I cummed all over his face, he enjoyed my cum; "I said dude you alright, I couldn't hold it." He answered, fuck yes, dijo que no te preocupes lo hiciste bien!

He never stops pleasuring me; it was the best feeling I have ever felt, mind blowing. I put my hard dick in his face, wiping my cum all over his lips, I pulled away and said, Daniel, I must go. He replied, wait. What? We are not done yet, did you like? I answered, Si!!

He asked me to do the same to him; He said kneel, I will put my hard boner into your mouth, like I did to you.

I pleasured him to what to me was an exceedingly long time, but my giving him my undivided attention, did not cause him to release; nevertheless, he seen to be really into it.

He stepped back away from me, his stiff boner stood out exceptionally long, pointed towards me. He asked could I put my boner in your ass hole, I'll first put on a condom? I said, fuck no dude. He said, Axel please try it for me, lie on your stomach, I will put baby oil between your ass cheeks and then I will put my hard boner slowly into you, your ass looks so good, nice, and round.

I did what he asked, I did not think I could continue it was very painful, I screened in ecstasy, I said please, Daniel, slower. He said OKAY, but Axel it feels so good, you're making me cum, I'm going to release! I asked, now? He said yes but hold on a few more minutes. He starts penetrating me more intensifying, pounding my ass; it starts to feel good, I asked him, Daniel, don't stop, I am releasing again! He asks, while I am inside of you, you are Cumming. I said yes, a big load in your bed. He yelled, (Impressive)!

I'll continue penetrating you while you release, my boner feels so good inside you. Axel, I am releasing now can you feel my heavy load? I answered, fuck yes dude. I felt so good, this experience was the best! Daniel me tengo que ir; (I must go).

He said no worries I got you! You came twice, what about me? I said if you hurry.

I changed positions, bent over, he examined my ass hole and put his tongue in my ass, I was trembling in excitement, he continued penetrating me, suddenly he pulled his dick amazingly fast out of my wet ass and yanked his condom off and begin ejaculating all over my ass, he was trembling and moaning as if it was electrifying, he screamed saying, Axel you're fucking awesome, he were breathing excessively loud; and said, you are the best Axel, we must do this again soon! I said OKAY, you liked it. He replied, yes dude I fucking loved it.

I got up from his bed he walked me to the bathroom, and kissed me and said, here is a towel to clean yourself up. He closed the door for me and said have at it unless you need my help? I answered, no dude I got this. I put my clothes on he walked me to the door, before I could walk out of the door, he pulled me back and asked me could I kiss you again before you go?

(This sexual experience was the best, I could never have imagined it),

I answered, I said, yes, then he said put your tongue in my mouth and he played with it until we were done, he said if we had more time, I would let you put your boner in my ass so you can explore new things, would you like that? I said yes, your brown ass looks good to me, oh yeah by the way, yes, I think you have a good-looking bod; you're going to let me fuck you someday? For sure dude.

I left going home, he said I could walk you home if you like. I said thanks dude, I'll be fine see you tomorrow. Oh yeah, Daniel do you still think you're not gay, you are so good at it? He replied if I am it's because of you, I'm evolving, (Evolucionando), recognizing who I really am. Which could be good for you; you need a man like me; Axel replied, y tu' Tambien, (you as well),

Once I made it home no one really missed me, accept Raymond, he asked jokingly, what took him so long! Pointing at my ass, Laughing. I went straight to the bathroom and immediately got in the shower; Heading home I stayed erect the entire time I could not resist the urge while showering to masturbate, because my mind stayed on Daniel pleasuring me. I worried was we moving too fast, was this a mistake, is he just a fucking football jock that's into fucking young guys.

Daniel approached me first which made me more confident in myself; My family makes me feel like I am perfectly queer, which gave me the feeling of being free to be me. (What freedom means to me is no fear); we all have our journeys, and this is Daniel's and mine.

Daniel had a girlfriend when we met; I don't feel she's completely over Daniel, based on how Daniel explained how he ended their relationship. One day their happy and a few days later I came on the scene, Daniel ends their relationship, spend most of his time with me every day; I know the last thing she would think about Daniel is that we're fucking.

The foreseeable problem is she could get in the way of our progress; Daniel will have to deal with that, that's satisfying for everyone.

He'll see being with me is not going to be easy in high school, unless he ends it with me because of all the pressure, which is a possibility; he changed his mind from being with Katy to being with me, why not again.

And then there is this; Daniel's parents seen to be doing well in their relationship, and their very accomplished and that's the way it's been all his life, their home is large and charming, they all drive new cars, travel, one of the best schools in Texas, Daniel has a bank card he can use when he wants to and always pay for everything for me when we go to the local Walmart and the mall.

My parents could tell a different story. My mother has been married all my life and have shown our family unparalleled love, worked hard to get us where we are without any help from our dad, he was like her extra kid.

I love dad because I was taught to love my father no matter what, but I'm extremely disappointed in him, he left us on our own, he betrayed us, I'm embarrassed of him.

I've never told Daniel that I'm in a government financial school assistance program that's why I'm in the same Preparatory School has him, I must keep my grades up, I'm required to keep an A+; nothing less, it pays for my entire education including college, our home was also granted via government.

I'm sure it doesn't matter to him; Daniel and I are going to do what it takes to graduate from high school together and go to college.

I'm enormously proud and grateful for my family we have been through a lot together, our leader kept her word, I'm going to become the man she expects. I am a young adult now; my young life has fulfilled its purpose, I like the fact that I have learned at an incredibly immature age who I am and my life's journey, young man developing from state of mind to another rapidly, and I am taking my first love with me, I am also glad I didn't get into a relationship with a girl, wasting her time and then I would have to explain why I seem to not really be into her.

My plans are to become a lawyer, because I think it's a good job security, it's highly paid, 100,000 per year, I like being challenged: After high school Daniel plans to become a pro athlete, we talked about what we're planning after high school we agreed to support each other and be friends always supportive totally loyal.

Daniel and I wasn't sure what kind of relationship we could have; we just knew we wanted to be together. We are unsure how this works, it was relatively easy for Daniel to make the transition and pursue me; his practice came from being with his girlfriend, in fact he said he'll see me as his girlfriend until he has a better understanding how this works. I thought that is a profound gesture; (it gives him the time to understand there's no gender identity necessary; we have the same equality, same sex couple, there is nothing that makes either of us more manly than what we are now). I had no experience at all, no one has ever mentioned sex to me it was not something we talked about in my family, I did some reading, it's not like hands on.

I looked forward to being with Daniel, sex with him is extraordinary, and we felt instant chemistry the first time we met.

Daniel is a head strong jock, but he's gentle with me; we have so much to learn about being gay and gay sex, but we are not going to put all the emphasis on sex. We are going to also focus on our education so we will be successful, our careers are as important, if not more important, we have to think about we'll need lots of money to give each other what we want together, as a couple. I realize like all relationships based on the relationship I experienced with my mom and dad, there will be problems and situations, the question is how we will deal with them.

Raymond is a part of this story, let's see how the dots connects for him. I am Raymond Kingston, I'm Axel's half-brother, we have the same last name because my mom was expecting me when she married. My dad is the only dad I've known, and I love him, I'm for sure he feels the same way about me. Axel and I grew up together and we're remarkably close, he's the family Prince; Axel is a very handsome person, he's not easy to overlook, he looks like dad; when we were boys, I felt I had to take care of him because I knew he were gay even before he was aware, we never talked about it, or sex because it just wasn't a big deal to me, I thought it could be too early for him, I wanted him to stay my little bruh; I stayed close to him so he wouldn't step out on his own. I knew a day would come for me to let him go to be himself; I decided to step aside, but with a close watch on him, Axel and I are close we were always together.

I was happy when he and Daniel became partners, glad it was Daniel, and he seems to be really interested in Axel. I knew other guys that were gay and out of the closet and some of them would come on to me, I didn't feel disrespected, and I even became friends with most of them.

One night a friend, Tim, called me and asked do I want to hang out, I said yes, because I was bored, I asked him would you like to meet, we'll go for a run? He said yes. Tim is a white dude, with brown hair and green eyes; we went to high school together, he lives with his parents for now, we talked a few times about our plans, he's a cool mate.

We met and ran a couple of blocks; he said let's get some rest so I can catch my breath. I said OKAY, so we walked, he asked me do you ever wonder why I don't have a girlfriend? I said no dude, I don't have a girlfriend neither; He said, well Raymond it's because I like guys, Raymond do you have a problem with? no dude, not at all. He asked what about you, have you ever thought about it. I replied, yes but not for sex, but for basic knowledge. He said Raymond you are a sexy man and if you asked me to give you some head, I would jump on it.

To my surprise I was getting a boner, he reached out and touch my boner and it got harder. I said dude I'm not into guys, don't touch me that way. Tim said your boner says something otherwise.

Raymond replied, I don't know why. Honestly, I really wanted him to give me a blow job, but I just didn't feel right about it. But I said let's go to the park and we'll talk more about you sucking my dick.

As soon as we were there, I wanted to get straight to it. I said, let's get this straight, I'm not gay, if I let you suck my dick no one can know and you can't let your feelings get involved, and it'll be the only time I do this with you, are you cool with?

Tim said no problem, it will never leave my lips. I pulled my jogging shorts down and took my swelled boner out and he start licking it slowly, I said Tim, put my balls in your mouth, he did; he got up and pulled his shorts down and his boner jumped out, he was wearing bikini underwear, his dick is so huge, it wouldn't stay in his pink bikini. I said, dude, you have a huge dick. (I was thinking to myself, it looked so appetizing).

He kneels again and continues sucking my dick, he was sucking my dick so good I needed to bust, he was jerking himself, with my boner in his wet hot mouth, suddenly I bust in his mouth, a massive load, he swallowed and junked up and shot cum on my leg, I felt the warmness dripping down my leg; I reached out to touch his boner, just to see what it felt like and I surprisingly kneel and begin sucking his dick while jerking myself off. Tim said, dude put my dick all the way into your mouth, keep sucking dude, you're fucking awesome, I wasn't expecting you to go this far. I put Tim's dick completely inside my mouth, his whole dick and jerking myself off fiercely, I stood up and shot my cum on his dick, we were moaning and trembling, we shot the same time.

He reached out to kiss me I said no dude this the end. Tim said, sorry dude, I said no worries. Tim, I must go, I'm trusting you'll never mention this to anyone, and this will never happen again. I enjoyed it, you were awesome, but it's just not who I am. Tim, do me a favor, don't call me again; I never want to put myself in this position again. No offense to you, Tim said none taken.

I jogged home with a new understanding about same sex, I also have more insight into whom my brother is, and more respect for the gay lifestyle, which is as normal as any lifestyle, But I'm not gay I just had a gay experience, which will not ever happen again, it's not in my journey.

Raymond kept the thought of Tim sucking his dick in his mind, he went home that night and wrote a song he plans to sing it to Axel someday, but he plans not to ever tell anyone about his experience with Tim, it's a need to know only.

Raymond is an impressive pianist, he practices with some of the best around town, he has his master's degree in music, is an African American Artist; with long dreads and a 11-inch cock, athletic physique.

Raymond's hopes, and prayers are for all gay people to come out of the closet and live a life of freedom, peace, and respect. After Raymond's gay sexual experience, he's going to encourage Axel to live his life free and in peace.

Tim goes on with his life, he realizes being open about himself with a guy he feels comfortable with, could be good for him, Raymond gave Tim a different view on things; He feels confident about love and the pursuit of his purpose. He doesn't see much of Raymond anymore; Raymond's busy he's planning to leave Texas and live in New York. Both; felt they enjoyed the experience and moved on with their lives.

Let's not forget about Michael, Axel first gay awakening, he and Raymond continued socializing they had music interest in common and would see each other at music events. Raymond was also aware of Michael's sexual orientation; Michael is now out of the closet, and incredibly happy with himself, he's in a relationship with a musician. Raymond believes that all men are equal, that they are endowed by their Creator with certain unalienable Rights, that among these are.

(Life, Liberty, and the Pursuit of Happiness).

"Our Future"

Chapter II

Daniel and I are still being intimate and have gotten closer, he's demanding but I allow it, I see potential in him.

Daniel Is extremely popular as a football player, six feet tall, weighs 145lbs, all muscle, deep brown Latino with short black hair, very masculine, intelligent, with an eight" boner.

I'm a very fit guy, intelligent, 135lbs, 6'3, African American, deep light blue eyes, Albano complexion, with long braids, unusual color that has been growing since birth, whiteish ten" boner. Daniel and I still doesn't consider we are a couple, per say; he was on the low; I called him today and I told him we won't be able to get together as much, because I need to focus on my school studies, it's exceptionally important I stay ahead. He wasn't happy to hear there's a limitation on the time I could spend with him; he said Axel meet me, we need to talk, I asked where do you want to meet? He said in the park behind the gym.

When I arrived, he was there waiting for me, he said we need to talk about our future. I asked, future, you meant your future? He answered, Axel! (Our future.) If we're going to be together we need to talk about how this will work, I understand you're busy and I'm proud to have an ambitious boyfriend.

It was during a weekday, so I was not expecting much; Daniel is a gentle guy, but unpredictable, sometimes I did not know what to expect when he was upset, but I was not afraid of him, his bark is worse than his bite, but he told me often he loved me, "I belong to him." To him that meant we were a couple.

He said, you understand I expect you not to be with anyone else; no sex with anyone only me, of course I'll do the same; you understand, right? I answered, yes, but, he said Axel no buts, please. I said Daniel does this mean I'm efficiently your boyfriend? I thinks so but I'm still not sure how this works, I'm going to treat you like you're my girl for now, it's not that you're like a girl it's that I've only been with a girl and never thought about being with a guy, I'll conclude soon, I won't make you wait too long. Axel asked, you want me to not see anyone until you decide? That's a big ask. Yes, you have a problem with? No, I'll do what you asked, but remember it's not just about you. Daniel said, of course not, I want require you to put me ahead of your studies, but I do expect you to make time for me. We have to spend time together, so we'll get closer.

He pulled me into his arms, holding me tightly, kissing me, we could feel each other's boner. "Do you want to go all the way?" He kneels, pulling my pants down and begin pleasuring me, with his finger going in and out of my perspiring ass hole, It felt so good I held my release so he would keep going as long as possible. Suddenly, I cummed in his mouth, he swallowed, I pulled him up, pulled my pants up and pulled him into my arms, kissing him, I said to him, Daniel, I love you. He replied, I love you as well.

We both left going home in different directions we were being discreet. I didn't care what people thought because my family loved me unconditionally, therefore there wasn't a reason for me to be discreet.

My parents taught us to always be ourselves, I have not said to my parents I am gay, but I will if ever asked.

Once, Raymond asked me Jokingly is Daniel my boyfriend? I respond, none of your business and besides, I'm not gay dude. Raymond said, oh, yeah right dude, of course not, you should be yourself. He said, I think I should tell mom you're gay. Raymond please don't tell her that; I don't want her to worry about me. Raymond went on to say, oh, by the way, mom wants me to keep an eye on you to make sure you are safe, I am responsible for you, don't get out of line little dude. We laughed, I respond, you're my security detail? I said, my brother, thanks good to know.

Raymond went on saying, Axel if you're gay I don't have a problem with, I love you no matter what. I want you to be happy, and I think Daniel is a nice guy for you. I respond, thanks dude, we are heading in that direction, but don't get ahead of yourself I'll keep you posted.

Daniel and I are in the same school, but we're in different buildings, we don't see each other until the end of the day, I wait for him in front of my building to pick me up and drive home together, I told Daniel we should tell everyone that we're spending time together studying on your math and science, I'm your tutor. Your dad pays me just like a job he wants me to help every day, and Daniel, it's the truth.

I have big plans for our future after high school, things are going well for us, no scandal so far; Daniel said, "Axel you are encouraging." I was glad to hear he wants to cooperate with my plans for us. It was a clever idea for Daniel to ask his dad to hire me as his math tutor, so that we could spend more time together without suspicion, we hangout shopping together it's always enjoyable, but there never seem to be enough time for us to be together.

When we want to be intimate, we go to Daniel's home because he has more privacy and at my home there's always someone there, we only socialize at my home, my mom were cool with.

Daniel's dad Pays me twelve dollars an hour I generally charged him for10 hours a week, I told Daniel thanks for that, Daniel wanted to be financially helpful, I was okay with that.

Daniel and I were growing closer and closer he felt comfortable with me, I also needed him to be dependable, secure with himself.

I did not see Daniel's brother much, but Daniel told me not to worry about his brother, he already suspects we are a couple it does not seem to matter to him, and he has never told their parents anything.

Daniel's mom is a young African American, Human Rights Activist, she is employed at Red Cross, sometimes she travels to other countries, married to a Mexican Immigrant, she also works for the Chamber of Commerce, responsible for fundraising.

Daniel looks more like his dad; his family is bilingual; they are a close upper class interracial family, wish was good for me, I speak Spanish, and two other languages, when I were around Daniel's parent's I spoke Spanish to impress his parents. (Daniely y yo hablamos Espanola junto's). At school no one understands us, we sometimes have open gay conversation with each other, we only do that for fun. His mom said, "I'm going to take you with me when I am traveling abroad, you're so impressive." I hoped she meant it. Paul works for his dad and spends most of his time with his older cousins.

The school and everyone were all new to me, Daniel knew most of all the students and faculty, no one makes me feel uncomfortable they were all friendly and nice to me. Daniel think the other students especially the guys, see me the way he does, in a sexual way. (Maybe, maybe not.)

Daniel and I was apart while in our classes for seven hours, once school ended I met him in front of my building like he asked, we drove home together, he said I missed you I was overly concerned how things were going for you. Did you meet anyone special today? I replied, no one why are you asking? He said, calm down dude I'm only asking, making conversation. I said, forgive me, it sounded like to me you expect me to meet someone in particular; He asked well did you? I answered, No.

He wanted to kiss me, there wasn't an opportunity; Our relationship is on the low; we're in love, committed to one another for now, however there are other guys that's appealing to me; maybe we're moving too fast.

We stopped at the local convenience store to get Slurpee's and parked, so we could talk before going home. Daniel mention again he had a girlfriend before me. He said, "I broke up with her a few days later after meeting you, when I knew I wanted to get to know you, hoped you would find me interesting;

Her name is Katy, she is our age, we have two classes together." I asked, did you see her today? He answered, yes and I will see her every day in class; But no worries it is over now, okay Axel? I said okay, is there anything else you want me to know? He answered I don't think so; I asked, have you ever been with a guy before me? No, I told you before, you are the first guy I ever looked at in a sexual way, and I see guys naked all the time. He asked, what about you? I answered yes, I was with a guy once, he only touched me and caused me to get an erection, it wasn't anything like us. Daniel asked, where is he now? I said, he and his family lives in West Dallas where my family and I moved from. Did he fuck you? I replied, No you the first, but at the time I kind of wanted him to. The difference between you and him, I didn't know him very well he's my brother's friend, you're my boyfriend, it's not like me being your girlfriend, acknowledge me for who I am; don't confuse it. Obviously, we have big dicks, dude it's an easy decision, we are gays; But no worries, we'll take care of one another like a couple, do you think we can do this? He answered, yep! I'll do whatever you want me to do, I just want us to be happy together. I replied, we are young men now; we're going to become men we must prepare. He said yes, good talk.

Axel I'm going to take you home now, I'll call you tonight before I go to bed.

Daniel, how about I speak to my mom tonight; I'll ask her will she have a small barbecue cookout this weekend so Raymond and I can invite our friends, we will just eat and socialize for a couple of hours. Daniel replied, that's a great idea, I will invite my mates, girls too and I'll ask my brother, Paul to come with. Great!

He pulled up in front of the house, I kissed him, got out of the car went into the house, took a deep breath, and exhaled, and yelled saying, hello family it's a wonderful day in the neighborhood.

Today is Friday, Daniel picked me up early for school because he has early football practice, and he plans to hangout tonight with his friends, they don't have a game this weekend, so he and his teammates decided to hang out together at the arcade.

I thought it was funny, having a boyfriend that's asking me do you mind if he spend time with his friends tonight. I didn't laugh but, I did tell him of course I don't mind. He then asked, what are you doing tonight? I answered, I'm going to hang out with Raymond at home we're going to play chess and watch a movie.

Daniel replied, Okay, sounds good, will your mom be there? I answered, I'm not sure. Daniel asked, Maybe I can call you later tonight I won't stay long with my mates, and you can come to my home? I said no, you stay out as long as you want, I'm going to catch up on some reading, besides, Raymond expects me to hang out with him. Daniel replied. Okay, than you call me first thing in the morning.

Sometimes I hang out with Daniel and his mates, but the guys looks at me in an uncanny way, I know I look eccentric, but there is nothing I can change about it, it's all natural born. Daniel doesn't particularly like me hanging out with him when he's with his mates, it makes him jealous and uncomfortable.

Daniel mentioned once, "Axel have you thought about getting the job that's available, front office assistant; so, you will be more approachable to some of the other students; They'll get to know you better, you're not that different from others, which will be good for us, we will have a perfect reputation to enter college, Right?" (That was his way of saying he don't like me around his mates.) I explained to Daniel; in college we can be together, as open as we want to be, or not.

Daniel and I spent a lot of time talking about our lives together. I asked him, have you made your mind up about playing football in college? "Yes, I plan to become a pro athlete." He likes the idea of dating someone with high ambitious. I told him I'm going to study law and become a Lawyer. all we must do is make it happen, our parents will be so proud and happy; I want us to do well and take care of one another, is it all possible, Daniel? "Yes, we are a team." (Daniel and I have a plan, but sometimes life takes a quick turn.)

Axel and I agreed to share our story together so I'm going to tell my view of our lives together. My name is Daniel Bernal, the son of a Mexican immigrant, our name means Blessed. I'm 18 years old, in the 12th grade; I will start by telling you how I committed to living up to my last name. Honesty. The truth is when I first saw Axel is when I saw him and his family earlier in the week moving in which took them about a week to finish.

I was so curious to know who they were, I live three houses away from them I can see when I stand in my driveway, a perfect view. I watched for a week mainly because I was curious about the tall dude with long braids, he's taller than I am; I used my binoculars without being noticed to get a better view. I was exceptionally curious; the next day I saw him standing on his porch I walked to their home, I first made sure I had an ink pen so maybe I'll be brave enough to ask for his number, to see if he would like to hang out with me, as I got closer, to my surprise he looked different from what I could see at a distance, I couldn't see the front of him, I only could see the side of him and the backside view. When I reached him, I could barely speak, his eyes were very noticeably light blue, the first thought that came to my mind was, wow, this is the most beautiful man I have ever seen.

A shockwave went through my body, I hoped he noticed the wave signal, it happened so suddenly.

I'm not sure whether I'm gay or not; That's going to take further examination, I had never felt this way before; I told him my name and asked where he moved from. He said west Dallas, I thought he would say, Johannesburg.

I knew right away I wanted to be someone special to him, I thought the best way for that to happen is to show I'm interested in him. Which, I have never thought about being with guys before I met Axel, I guess it's something that I've felt deep inside; I was so turned on, I couldn't believe it.

I do expect I'll have to tell my family about what I have found out about my sexuality, we I've never kept secrets from one another, but not now because I want to be sure Axel really wants to be with me.

I have conflicting emotions I'm still interested in girls, sometimes in classes I get a huge erection looking at the girls, I feel it could be a problem for me fighting the urges. I want to keep my agreement I made with Axel to only have sex with each other. That's the foreseeable problem. I'm not saying I won't surrender to my urges, but, I'm not, not saying it.

When I tell my mom she should be understanding, as an activist she's into humans rights, the right to choose, equality, Democrat versus Republican, you know the important concerns people are fighting for these days.

Then there's the Higher Education Preparatory School, I'm close to most of the students and faculty, I want my mates to accept and treat Axel with respect the same as I'm treated; they are genuinely nice people; I want Axel to enjoy high school and not moved to home schooling before he goes to college, I'm sure Axel can take care of himself, but high school could be difficult for him.

(I have Secrets that I have kept for some of my mates that will give me leverage. As a football quarterback team leader, I don't think anyone wants to be a problem for me, and besides, Axel is a very friendly, talkative person, easy to be around. Some of my mates are not as heterosexual as appear to be, I walked up on two of my mates jerking off, standing in front of each other getting off looking at one another's dicks, they were into each other.)

Axel is profoundly serious about his freedom to be himself and not have to explain about his naturally unusual appearance, so hopefully he'll bring that vibe to the others.

Nevertheless, he will always have his bodyguard, Raymond, and me to protect him. For me, my parents made sure I understood to accept people for who they are, no exception; I never thought it would be me that needed to be accepted.

Axel has an attraction that could calls others to find him sexually attractive, even the girls. That's my fear and insecurity that I will have to deal with on my own.

Axel has brought to my mind to be a mature young man, not just a dude in high school without a clue, he emphasizes we are just steps away from college and that's where adulthood starts, we need to think like adults.

My ex-girlfriend Katy she is mature also smart and pretty, but not enough to keep me interested in her as a girlfriend and we only had sex once and we decided not to ever have intercourse again because we didn't use contraceptive, the last thing she or I want to happened is for her to get pregnant. So, technically before Axel I was a virgin.

I find Axel to be a good catch, looking forward to Axel and I Journey to pursuit our happiness and a successful life, and I love that he speak Spanish as well.

I want to be clear. I decided to be with Axel by choice, what's concerning is how was I able to jump from male to female so easily, that's why I say I'm not sure if I'm gay, but Axel is convinced I am; it sounds like I'm more like bi-sexual it also could mean I'm bi-curious.

More importantly, Axel and Katy deserves the best, both trusted me to be the first, which means they both open their hearts to me. Katy is a very desirable and a lovely lady, but I feel more connected to Axel, sex with him was a phenomenal experience, for both of us, Now all I do is think about how I can make him happier; he is the best thing that any guy should want to be with. I don't want to become overbearing, it's the jock in me, I think hopefully I'll be able to find a book in the library on the life of same- sex couples.

This is all new to Axel and me, we have lots of unanswered questions, I want to do my part and find more information on how it works. I want Axel to be happy being with me, I'm glad I got to him first.

Axel surprised me with exciting news, he asked me, Daniel are you ready, tomorrow we're having the BBQ we talked about. Is Paul coming with? I answered yes. "Be here at 7pm."

My friends and I arrived on time like Axel ask, the backyard is perfectly manicured, everyone was out except Axel, he was still getting ready. His mother approached us first, she said hello guys, thanks for coming. I said, we're happy to be here, your home is so beautiful as always. Ms. Kingston thanks for the invite. She said, you all are very welcome, Axel will come out in a few minutes. I said ok. Raymond offered drinks; I said, yes thanks dude.

We all sat down, Axel appeared, I almost wanted to get up and kiss him; He said, hello Daniel, I see you brought Paul and the others; Hey Paul, thanks for coming. Paul replied, Hi Axel, it's nice to see you, you are as beautiful as always.

Everyone laughed, Axel said, thanks Paul I'm glad you noticed; Axel said, Daniel your brother has jokes. I got the feeling Paul wasn't joking, he had a look in his eyes as if he were undressing Axel, I thought to myself, I wonder what's on Paul's mind.

Raymond, Paul, and the guys started throwing a football back-and-forward to each other, I thought, cool they hit it off fast. Axel and I sat down with Ms. Kingston, and we all talked for about 45 minutes, and some of the guys sat around us laughing and talking with us. Everything was going so well; his mom was so nice to us.

Axel said to his mom, is it okay to show Daniel my room, when we come down we'll be ready to eat? His mom answered, of course it's okay, but hurry.

This is the part where it gets intense; I looked around quickly, Axel's started kissing all over me very forcefully, I thought, oh my god this is impressive. His home is large with four bedrooms, perfectly decorated, I responded by holding him tightly in my arms. He said, Daniel we must go down and eat are you ok do you think this is impressive, are you happy to be here? I kissed him and said let's go and eat, I'm hungry, you are causing my dick to get hard. Axel replied, okay, my dick is hard too, we don't want others to notice, but will you kiss my dick really quickly and just lick the head with your tongue? Daniel said okay, take it out, I did, Daniel opened his mouth wide, and I put my precummed dick in his mouth and he sucked my dick, suddenly he stopped and said let's go down now, we don't want anyone to catch us. Axel replied, okay dude, thanks for the quickie.

We ate relatively fast, everyone was so hungry it didn't take us long to finish eating, everything was great the BBQ was so good, I kind of hated to leave, everyone said their goodbyes, Axel's Mother surprisingly kissed me on the cheek and said, thanks for coming, Paul I'm sure I see you again soon? Paul answered, yes ma'am, copy that.

(When we left I start to think, it feels like Axel, and I are a couple.)

The next day Axel calls me to my surprise, a few days later and asked is it a suitable time for me to come by? I said you can always come, remember you're my tutor, that's our coverup; come now I'm alone, I don't expect anyone to come home, maybe in two hours you're fine.

He arrived and said let's go to your room, as soon as we enter the room he started undressing me and said I need you now, could I make love to you my way? I said yes, But I hope it's not too painful; (Axel said, I'll go easy on you, but I am a little stressful today.) You're going to need lube, I'll get some, I reached under the bed hoping I wouldn't need to leave the room to get lube, it was under the bed like I hoped, sometimes I get horny at night, I jerk off to get some sleep.

I gave it to him, he start removing his clothing; I looked at him admiring his beautiful body, while he's putting on a condom; Axel's body is pale, it's two toned, he's slim, he's has straight blond hair on his chest, the same around his long fattish cock, it's whitish.

(He looks so different from anyone I have ever known.)

He told me to lie down and hold your legs in the air. I did; he put the lube inside of me deep with his finger, it felt good he went on with the process by entering me slowly, once he was in me, he penetrated me a little forcefully it was okay it felt good, he's fucking freaky in bed.

Then he stopped and pulled out and moved up sitting on my chest, rolled his sweaty balls and wet ass hole in my face, I licked his ass hole, he moaned, Don't stop it feels good, expressing pleasure, he said fuck dude you liked licking my ass hole, it feels good continue; Than he played with his dick in my face and said dude you like this dick, put your finger in my ass hole, I fingered him slowly, he's moaning, squeezing his butt cheeks around my finger, he were trembling, his long whiteish cock in my face, then he begin lowing his body and went into my ass again, penetrating me extremely hard, I said Axel slow down, he continue pounding my ass I screamed in ecstasy, louder and louder, It was awesome!

Axel asked, are you enjoying this, then stop complaining, don't tell me to slow down; I'm Cumming you're interrupting the flow. (Fuck dude,) this is what I thought about all day, you need to focus, so you can please me; He pulled me up again, kissing me with his tongue deep in my mouth, forcefully. He looks at me and said I love you, but don't ever tell me to stop, that's not what I like hearing while fucking you, you should be saying how much you love me, keep fucking me, my ass belong to you; You have much to learn about me, you do what I say without any hesitation.

After that, then he said get me a towel, I'll clean up and leave. I asked are you upset? he said, what do you think? You say you love me and would do what I say, now you're fucking complaining, I must go, you need to think about what you really want; I'm a man, you should expect to get fucked hard I'm not your fucking girlfriend, you should've realized by now. I'll see you tomorrow. Please pick me up on time, I have a meeting to attend. Thanks: I love you.

I said really. He answered, of course dude don't be fucking foolish. He left without me walking him to the door. I didn't know what had just happened.

This is a side of Axel I had never seen; I see I have much to learn, this is when I first felt like I am a gay person. I felt like Axel dominated me; No one has ever treated me that way, I know Axel has deep feelings for me, maybe he just wanted to prove a point. I still look forward to being with.

The next day I picked Axel up early so he'll be on time for his meeting, which he has meetings with staff regularly, he also assist, tutoring for three teachers. I knew he would be great, he's also exceedingly popular with the students even with some of my mates, some of my mates are only in the football program because of Axel tutoring club. All I hear is good things about him, I know he has a lot on his mind, I hoped he'll talk to me about last night, I don't want to be pushy because it could be a combination of things, including home stuff.

I eloquently Asked, Axel are you okay? He said, yes, are you? I said thanks for asking, dude, should we talk about what happened last night? He answered, we fucked! What, you have a problem with you need to understand I'm busy doing my job at the school and doing my own studies, sometimes your job is to only help me relieve stress, you might have to be fucked hard, maybe you should go back to Katy, a simpler life, what do you think about that dude?

Oh, I'll catch the bus home after school, I'll be late, I've been assigned to help a guy catch up, I will call you tonight. Okay Axel, your right I should fucking reconsider dude. Sarcastically, He said Right; Thanks Daniel, I love you, I'll call you later. Bye, have a good day.

I can't believe that just happened, being with a guy seem to be complicated, It's nothing like being with a girl, I'm a football star, with a boyfriend that's demanding, not easily pleased, or satisfied.

I need to let him know I'm not happy with the way he is treating me maybe he will come to his senses, because I'm trying to be open-minded so we can graduate as a couple and attend Southern Methodist University together. I hope that's what he still wants.

I don't like the fact that he tutors so many guys, someone else may become interested in him, you know; boys will be boys, Axel is always horny and could be tempted, he's so beautiful and perfectly queer and hard to resist.

Axel called me after he made it home from school, he call to apologize, I hoped he would so we can continue living the life together as planned. I have accommodated Axel' I deals and ready to move forward and besides, there will be many more situation outside of our relationship, he must remember no one knows but us; If we keep it concealed until we graduates it will be much easier.

I'm sure Paul and Raymond are convinced we're a couple. (No worries, they love us and will never betray us.)

I couldn't resist the idea, so I had to asked, "would you like to come over, I have a couple hours to spare, and I could use a massage, my legs are aching?" Axel answered, no doubt, I missed you. I hurried to clean my room, because Axel will say, "dude you're a fucking mess." He came to the back door, and I opened the door, he came in and said, hey, you look and smell great, did you clean up for me?

Axel is way beyond his years, he's a gentleman, his parents did well. How did your tutoring go? "Oh, good, his name is David he's in the 12th grade, I think he's catching up, he also needed to complete his resume." I didn't want to rush into it, but I wanted to have sex, I wanted him to make the first move.

I sit down on my bed, he sat at the desk chair in front of me, he said, "takeoff you pants, tell me where you're stiff I'll start there, massaging one leg at a time." I said okay. He massaged my legs for a few minutes, I got a boner, I said will you put my boner in your mouth while you at it, he answered, whatever you want to do I'm here to make it up to you. I kissed him, he held me so tightly I could feel his muscles; I'm tall, but Axel is taller, lean, and all muscles.

He ask, "which part you want first?" He started touching me all over my body, I was touching his long thick wooly braids, he asked do you want me to pleasure you? I said take it out, he did and begin very slowly pleasuring me, it felt so good, he kept going, he asked do you want to go all the way? I said yes, he knew where to find the lube, he asked, put the lube in me with your finger first and put on a condom, I see you have some on the table, where you planning to fuck me, or you had someone else in mind?

I said, no talking; he took off his clothes and said, "put lube as far up in me as you can and keep pushing in with your finger, get the lube as far in me as possible, my ass is tight;" he laid on his back and put his long legs up on my shoulder, before I went into him, he said lick my ass hole like you did before, I did what he asked with the quickness, I made him extremely wet and greased, He said, "dude fuck me;" I put my stiff cock into him, his ass hole is pretty, it's whiteish like his cock, he said, "go for it Daniel", I'm penetrating him slowly he start moaning as if I'm pleasing him, I lower his legs some so he could jerk off while I'm in him, that turns him on.

I said don't bust, wait for me. He moaned more like he was about to bust I said hold on Axel we're going to bust together. I pulled out slowly, started masturbating, we bust the same time I shot all over his chest, he shot far up in the air, and some hit me in the face, we were both panting like animals. He asked, "do you want more?"

I answered, can you penetrate me? "he said look at me I'm still stiff, just imagine me as your fucking machine, you tell me what you need, I'll cater to you."

He picked up the lube from the floor and put a big finger full of it on his fingertip and put his finger far up in me, I'm lying on my stomach. He put on a condom; He went into me slowly until he was all the way in, penetrating my wet booty hole for about 12 minutes and pulling his long cock in and out rapidly, I wanted to cry, then he released a massive load into his condom, I could feel the heat from his cum, he pulled out and collapsed on my back breathing hard. Once we were done he said, let's get up and clean up before someone comes home. We did and he said walk me to the door, I did as he was leaving, He said, "no more fighting dude," I said ok, I'll see you tomorrow. Bye!

Axel me dijo mientras su polla está en mi jugoso culo, hablando con un tono suave, besándome el cuello, con su larga polla gorda en mí. "Voy a hacerte el amor tanto que tu mente no te dejará pensar en nadie más que en mí, eso incluye a Katy".

(Axel told me while his cock were in my juicy ass, speaking in a soft tone, kissing my neck, "I'm going to make love to you so much that your mind won't let you think of anyone but me, that includes Katy.") He has a way with words.

For the first time Axel and I are going out to dinner after school with two of my mates that Axel invited, they are students at our school, Axel is their tutor. That sounds great he's the host, but I will pay, I like spoiling Axel, I can afford it and I don't want him to spend his money on bull shit things like going out to eat with me, and our friends. The objective is to mingle with other's trying to make life for us as normal as possible, I'm going to drive us there we will meet the guys there at 5 o'clock, we're going to meet at a popular hamburger joint in Deep Ellum, Downtown Dallas.

I were thinking to myself apprehensively; I trust Axel but I feel he could become interested in other guys, there are lots of dudes here in our school, based on what I can see is interested in Axel, he don't hang out with them but I know given a chance they will make conversation with him, hoping to get him to hang out, it's not that Axel appeared to be gay if there's a such, it just that Axel has a very appealing look about himself and it wouldn't take much for someone to become attracted.

Axel is a mature young guy, he is a college undergrad, he confront responsibilities head on, I never want to be faced with the threat of losing him, I also feel I'm more committed than he is, I'm kinda afraid he's going to fuck someone else other than me I'm not sure how I would manage it, I'm sure I'll want to kick his ass; I understand we're new at this, especially Axel, because he has never been in a relationship; now that I'm out to myself, occasionally I see guys that I find desirable; I get a boner looking at them without being noticed..

Nevertheless, I love Axel with my whole heart, I'm committed to Axel, if it were possible I would ask Axel to marry me, instead, I'm going to ask him to exchange rings that symbolize us as a married couple, maybe he'll feel more committed to me, I'm not worry about my mates asking why Axel and I are wearing gold bands, our relationship is too important to be embarrassed.

I must admit, the thought has crossed my mind to fuck someone other than Axel, just to see how it feels, but It'll take an incredibly special dude to get me in bed and besides Axel gives me everything I need, we're one in bed, whatever it takes, we don't hold back.

"Turning Point"

Chapter III

We all arrived at the Downtown hamburger joint the same time, we sat at a booth, I wanted us to sit face to face making eye contact; my dad says the best conversation starts with eye contact.

Jamal, Fabian, Daniel, and I Went to the counter to order our food, Daniel ordered first, he told the rest of us to order whatever you want I'll pay. Axel said, thanks Daniel, but it's my idea, so let me pay. Daniel replied, Axel, no problem It's my treat. Fabian said thanks dude it's on me the next time. Jamal asked, are you all fighting over who'll pay the bill? You sound like my parents when they go out with their friends; Daniel answered, No it's on me. Jamal said, Axel we have a pool at my home I can give you my phone number, you can call me sometimes and I'll pick you up and we'll go to my house to swim. Daniel asked only Axel? Jamal answered, you all are welcome; I thought Axel would like to hang out with me sometimes, we can become close friends.

Jamal is a young African American he's on the football team, he's tall and incredibly good looking; Fabian Is Latino, not so tall but he does play sports, he's also good looking and popular, chess champion; there in classes with Daniel.

Jamal asks Daniel, where did you and Axel meet? Daniel answered, I live on the same street as Axel, he went on asking, do you stay overnight together sometimes, Daniel quickly answered, No.

Jamar said I'm allowed to have overnight stays, Axel I have my own room, I said OK, I'll call sometimes when I want to get away from home.

(To Axel that meant he want him to fuck him in his sculptured round ass.)

(Jamal wasn't so talkative when we studied alone, therefore I was surprised; I said thanks Jamal for the invite, I'm glad you feel free to open up to me, this is how we all can become closer friends.)

Daniel changed the conversation To Sports, I felt Jamal under the table touching my foot looking at me with a smirk on his face. I thought Daniel would notice but he didn't seem to notice, he continue talking about his upcoming games, which is not why we were there; Jamal continue touching me, I was getting a boner while he's touching my foot, it felt weird, I wasn't for sure whether it was intentional or not.

Fabian asked me do you play sports Axel? I answered, sometimes for fun, I like basketball; he said it's obvious you are very tall; Do you have a girlfriend? I said no.

(I start to think he's fishing for information, if I put my big whitish dick in his mouth, he'll stop fucking being so inquisitive.)

(I was thinking to myself, I would like to put my big whiteish cock in Jamal tight asshole and Fabian Watch me screw his best bud.) I think this might not have been such a clever idea after all; we all had the look on our faces as if we were curious about one another, I want us all to become friends, not fuck amigos.

(Maybe it's normal for young men to be horny all the time, have fucking on their minds constantly, for me just the simple touch in certain situations I'll get a boner, I love having sex.)

As we were leaving, Jamal said wait Axel here's my phone number, he gave me the paper with his number on it, he touched my finger, looking in my eyes sincerely; it was surely a silent invitation to his ass, at least that's the way I saw it.

When Daniel and I got in the car he said dude you have a boner, did you do that on purpose? I answered what are you talking about? He said correct me if I'm wrong, it seems to me Jamal has the hots for you, did you know? No, of course not. You ever talked to him about sex when you were alone with him? No. Will you call him sometimes? I said, maybe but probably not, next question Daniel, if you like, I'll asked him could you come with, if that makes you more comfortable, we could all stay over together, maybe we can all sleep in the same bed, dude that'll be cool.

Daniel said, Deja de bromear, lo digo en serio amigo.

Axel respond, Por supuesto que lo Eres ca'lmate. (Calm down dude.) Daniel while I'm at school, working or studying no one ever looks or directly approach me as if I'm queer in a gay kind of way, I've learned things in the last year I can manage most guys' situations; I think I'm smarter than most guys at our school, so I don't really think you need to worry you're my only interest, you're my future just trust me.

Daniel respond, maybe Jamal and Fabian planned it? Axel said, that's fucking absurd, don't over think it, I invited them, I'm glad you didn't say anything hostile; It's like a chess game Daniel, always think three moves ahead of your opponent. Daniel said, Axel, I expect you to be responsible, this relationship has gotten profoundly serious for me. Axel respond, oh, okay, before now it's just a test drive. Axel don't be ridiculous dude I'm just trying to make sure we're on the same page, you don't get distracted. Daniel, please understand I'm still a young dude it's going to take a little time to get all my ducks in a row. Daniel asked, Axel, are you still into me the way you were when we first met? If not, I could slow it down for you to catch up? Thanks dude I'll keep you posted. Dude, take me seriously, unless you're already distracted, that's what we should be talking about? Daniel, I got you, don't worry.

We continue talking while driving home, I asked Daniel how is Katy, have you spoke with her? Yes, she's doing fine; we only say hello. Axel asked, how does that feel?

Honestly, it was just a year ago, she and I was close kissing all the time and holding hands but now we just say hello and keep walking, which doesn't feel so good, I feel like I lost a friend. I said to Daniel I understand. I think you should manage it the way you think is best, I trust you. Do you ever think about having sex with her again? No, it wasn't what I call sex, but to answer your question, all I ever think about is making love to you, I told you, you are important to me, I just want us to stay on course.

We arrived at my home, I said, thanks for everything; Daniel said, no problem, Axel, did you have an enjoyable time with me and our mates? Axel answered, yes, we can do this again, and I'll bring Raymond with, and by the way dude, I don't like you always insistent on paying my way, I don't have money like you, but I can pay my own way. Daniel said, Axel I'm just trying to be helpful. Okay Axel if you insist, I look forward to us doing it again, and you can pay the tab if it makes you happy, I'll bring my mates to hang out with, we could go to a place like Hunky's on Cedar Springs. (They're laughing.)

(Hunky's is a popular restaurant in a gay community.)

I kissed him and said goodbye, I'll see you tomorrow morning. Axel wait, what are you going to do with your boner? What boner? you ruined it; take a shower, we can't fuck every day, it isn't the right time for me. Daniel replied, ok I'll see you tomorrow.

I enter the house; I said hello, my mom said hi there, how are you? Axel answered, I'm fine mom. My mom said, I'm glad you're here I want to talk to you.

She said, Raymond is going to New York City, to attend Juilliard Art school to study music, He will be there only for one year. Axel said wow, this is updated news.

He didn't want me to mention it before he was accepted. Axel asked, where is he now? He's out shopping with some of his friends. Do you think Raymond will have time to teach me to drive so I could drive us a round, to replace him? No, he won't have time to teach you, I'm going to enroll you in a Drivers Ed Course, I'll keep you posted. Good, can you get that done as soon as possible, I would like to get my license before I go to college? Okay son, Let's go over our plans and talk about what things are going to look like for you in a few months.

I am going to have a sendoff party for Raymond, he's a great young man, and a wonderful pianist. (Ms. Kingston thought to herself, I'm so glad my sons genuinely love one another, unconditionally.) Raymond said he's going to perform tomorrow, he said he's going to do a dedicated performance for us. Axel said that's impressive, I look forward to it.

Ms. Bernal called to offer her caterer at no charge to me, I accepted her offer, Her and her husband won't be able to make it but we're planning to meet soon, we talk over the phone often but hasn't had time to meet in person.

She's a nice person; proud of her sons, and she told me she's happy our sons are good friends.

Ms. Kingston went on saying, Axel, you are accepted to go to SMU for 4 years; I was contacted by the government assistant program, and they explained the terms to me. Axel said, I'm excited, tell me more mom!

you'll live in an apartment not far from the campus, you'll need to go to work, work a few hours a week to help with your household expenses, I'm going to pay your rent every year, and I'll give you a bank card for emergencies. Wow, mom that's so nice of you, SMU is exactly where I want to go!

Axel, you will need to be as focus as you are now, keep your grade average up, it's a requirement; College is a lot more challenging, it's good you're taking first-year classes now, which puts you ahead in some of your studies.

Daniel's mom told me Daniel is going to SMU as well, so hopefully you could spend time together in college like you're doing in high school. Axel asked, mom how do you like Daniel? She answered, he's great and I'm glad you all are friends; Do you all get along well? Yes, he's my best friend.

Does he have a girlfriend? No ma'am. What about you are you interested in anyone? No. She said, no worries I'm sure you will find someone, it's not a big deal, there's no reason to rush. You are happy with yourself and that's what matters, I'm sure it hasn't been easy to be you, but son you have made it look easy.

Mom, will you unbraid and style my hair, cut it shoulder length, I want a trendier look for college. Okay, we can do it now.

Axel's mom unbraided, and washed his hair, cut a bob style, and then blow dried it straight, she said, okay Axel take a look. Axel said, mom, I love it. She asked is it too long? No mom, I love it. Axel mom said good, now you look like a businessperson. We'll go shopping this week, so you can get what you need for college before all the good stuff are gone, you'll need to by some new clothes as well. Mom, will I need to get a roommate? She said, no, you and I will do it all ourselves.

Axel said great! Mom, I love you so much, thanks for taking loving care of me. Axel's mom said you are very welcome, and I wouldn't have it any other way; you are my son, and you matters.

I want you to feel you can come to me about anything, you have been a good son and I trust you completely, you will have to make some crucial decision about yourself and there are no one that can make them for you. I know you'll always do the right thing, like your dad and I taught you.

Axel, do you drink alcohol? No ma'am, but I plan to with Daniel after graduation. Mom asked, why Daniel? He's my partner; I trust he won't let anything happen to me.

Axel, your dad has a problem with alcohol, he's allergic to it; I want you to be careful if you do have a drink, it could be hereditary.

That's what I meant, if you have any situation, whatever it is remember, your brother and I will always be here for you. Raymond loves you and want the best for you; we are all in this together.

Do you ever think about your dad? Yes ma'am I do, maybe he'll come to see us soon?

He loves us, he just needed to get professional help. Axel said, I love him too and hopes he gets the help he needs; I was angry at him for leaving, but his mental health is especially important, he's a good man and we're close; I hope he feels the same about me, I forgive him. Thanks mom for the update, good talk.

Hold on son, there's more. Tomorrow, two people with the caterer will do the serving but I want you to help. There's going to be a lot of people here, including some of the faculty from your school and we want everyone to feel comfortable. Okay mom, awesome, just let me know what you need done.

Mom, do you mind if I go out now with Daniel? No, you can go, please don't be out too late.

I called Daniel, and said Dude, I'm heading your way, Daniel said, okay, what's up? You'll see when I get there.

I arrived, Daniel asked why did you cut your hair? My mom did. She unbraided my hair, washed and blow dried it straight. You like? Yes, you look so different. Is that good or bad? Actually, I love it, you look like a preppy guy now, Axel said, trust me Daniel that's not my intent.

You asked her to cut it in that style? Yes. Daniel asked, you don't think it looks feminine? fuck no dude, I want a fresh start; I want to look more professional. Daniel said I'm going to get my hair cut in a fresh style too. Axel said OKAY, not too short I like your hair the way it is.

Axel, I'm going out tonight with some friends I'll call you later tonight or tomorrow.

Axel said OKAY, have a fun time, I'm going to stay home and do some reading, have fun.

Daniel went out with his best mates, Axel was home reading, Paul called, He said, Hello Axel, Axel said, hello, is this you Paul? Paul said, yes.

Axel asked, what's up, did something happened to Daniel?

No, I called because I'm bored. Axel asked, dude how can I help? Paul answered, you can have dinner with me so we can talk. Axel said, Paul that's not a good Idea. Paul said probably not, but I know a wonderful place, I would like to treat you. (Axel thought to himself, damm, why me, if he offers me his ass, I won't be able to resist.)

He said, okay Paul come now, hurry so no one will see us spending time together alone. Okay Axel, I'll pick you up at the end of our street. As soon as Paul could see Axel in the car, he said, Axel you look so damm good! I love your hair cut, why did you do it? Axel replied, thanks dude, I want to look more businesslike, for college.

Axel said, Paul this is a really bad idea, I can't believe we are doing this. What gave you the ideal it's okay to call me? Paul answered, I've planned to a while ago, you're a fucking cool ass dude. Axel said, dude what are you talking about? Get to the point or else I'm not going anywhere with you.

While driving, Paul said, do you like sea food? Axel replied, yeah dude, but did you really call me for that? Or you want me to fuck you, that's why you call? Paul said, fuck yes dude; Axel asked, you're not worry about Daniel? Paul answered, not at this moment, are you? Axel said, yes, I love Daniel, I don't want him to get hurt, I'm sure you agree, right?

Paul said, yes, so this will be our secret forever, but we can't deny what we're feeling at this moment. Axel have you ever looked at me in a sexual way? No, I meant maybe. Paul said, so I'm sexy to you and you want me as well, I can get us a motel room. Axel asked, you can? Let's go.

Paul and Axel went to a hideaway, nice small cabin near the lake a few miles away from their home. Axel said, this is a lovely place, is it expensive, you've been here before? Paul said, yes, this is the place I bring girls I've dated. Axel replied, really.

Paul, I really love Daniel, it's just that I have a problem with saying no, I'm always horny and I need to control myself, I'm sure if Daniel finds out he will break up with me.

Axel went on and said, as for you, you might not ever get over having sex with me, I hear I'm good at it. Paul asked, you're having sex with other guys now? Axel respond, I'm always thinking about it and there are so many guys at my school and in the neighborhood that's gay, but their undercover, kind of like you.

And it's not hard to entice me; I am a young man, and I wasn't prepared, my family and I have never talked about sex, I'm learning as I go. Daniel is learning as well, we agreed to learning only with each other, I have a problem with that concept. Kind of like now. No worries, Daniel and I use condoms, and most everyone we know.

Paul we can choose not to do this. Paul said, Axel relax and have a drink, Axel said, I don't drink alcohol, and you shouldn't either, because you're driving. Paul said, okay no problem.

Paul leaned froward, kissed Axel, passionately massaging Axel's lower belly, "he said let's get comfortable," Axel removed his shirt and then pulled Paul into his arms and turned him around, boning Paul's ass. Paul said, Axel this is something I've never done, so you will need to lead me, and I'll follow. Axel asked, why do you find me irresistible? Paul answered, you're different from anyone I have ever met, you fucking hot, and sexy.

Axel went on asking, so that's why you want me to fuck you, because I look different, that's your answer? Paul said, exactly.

Jokingly Axel said, I find you irresistible because your booty hole keeps calling my name, I'm going to see what I can do about that, I have noticed you looking at me and my thoughts were, I would like to fuck you in your ass. What do you think about that Paul? Paul replied, show me what you're talking about, I'm ready.

Axel, while boning Paul's ass, kissing his neck, Paul said, Axel I can feel your boner pressing against my mi culo. Axel asked, do you like it? he reached to Paul's belt buckle and slides his pants down and Paul didn't have on any underwear, Axel begin kissing around Paul's ass hole putting his finger in and out of Paul's ass hole slowly, Paul breathing loudly, he said, Axel slow down I'm not a bottom.

Axel said, Paul fuck that; you are who I need you to be; I'll let you fuck me, but I like being the aggressor.

Paul said, but I could jerk you off. Axel said I can do that to myself, if we're going to do this, I'll need to put my dick in your ass hole, and you'll need to cooperate.

Paul kneel, suck my dick like the girls sucks yours. Paul start licking Axel's nippers and went down to Axel' cock and sucked Axel Huge dick, Axel said get it wet dude, keep sucking, he asked Paul, did you bring condoms, Paul said yes and lube too, Axel asked, give it to me, Paul reached and got a package with everything we will need.

Axel asked, where did you get this it's so convenient, Paul said a gay bookstore. I read a book about gay sex, so I picked up a few items. Axel said, fucking awesome dude, keep sucking my fucking dick, keep my dick in your mouth.

Axel going in and out of Paul's mouth, holding Paul's chin so that Paul couldn't pull back. Paul drooling from his mouth, Axel pulled out of Paul's mouth and tongued him deeply.

Axel whispered in Paul's ear, saying are you ready dude, concentrate on my dick, not the pain.

Lie on the bed with your legs in the air, Axel begin sucking Paul's dick, drooling down his dick, putting Paul's dick deep in his throat; Paul Moaning, you are amazing dude. Axel squirt lube between Paul's ass, he said damm, my dick is so hard, I'm going to go in now, he did, and Paul start moaning, Axel, I'm fucking Cumming dude, Axel said, we just got started, but good enjoy yourself. Paul said, this feels so awesome and you are fucking good at it, keep fucking me dude.

(Axel doesn't say anything, he's' thinking to himself, Paul ass is fucking good and tight, better than Daniel's and some of the others.)

Tears rolling down Paul's face and Axel lowered Paul legs and came out, kiss Paul with his tongue deep in Paul's mouth, he stopped and said turn over Paul.

Paul did, Axel slowly went in Paul's ass and fucked him like a dog. Paul said, dude tell me you love me, this isn't anything like I could have imagined, dude, this is the best sex I have ever had; how do you feel? Axel said I feel like, you love my dick and that's what matters to me, pleasing you. Paul stopped Axel causing Axel's dick to pop out, Axel trying to put his dick back into Paul's ass, Paul moving his booty hoe, so Axel has to chase it with his dick, Axel desperately trying to get back into

Paul's asshole he said, dude stop running from this dick, this is what you wanted, hold still.

Paul asked, will you spend time with me again sometimes, I don't know how I'm going to be able to resist you, how I will make this our only time, Axel you have been on my mind, and I jerk off thinking about you all the time. Axel said stop talking, I need to bust this fucking load, we will talk later.

Axel begins fucking Paul ridiculously hard, he said turn over Paul, I'm going to bust in your throat, Paul quickly did as Axel order. Axel yelled loudly saying Fuck dude why are you doing this to me? Paul said I love you, with Axel's cum rolling down Paul's lips, Axel kissed licking the cum, putting his tongue in and out of Paul's mouth.

Axel stopped and went to the restroom to get them a wet towel. He wiped himself up and went to Paul, Paul seemed exhausted, Axel wiped Paul up, and wiped Paul face very gently and said dude you are fucking amazing. Paul said suck my dick again and make me cum.

Axel sucked and Paul cummed and was lying on his back, and he shot cum everywhere Axel watching, he said, I have never seen anyone fucking cum so much. Paul said, "this is what you did to me." (Paul cummed like a stream of pee.)

He got up and they got dress and held each other, Axel said not a word of this can ever be spoken; while Kissing Paul, licking Paul's face, and lips.

Paul said, but truly Axel, my brother is too immature for you, maybe you should rethink it. I can do more for you; I'm going to buy a home, I'm going to take over my father's business, you could live with me while going to college. Axel replied, Yeah, right, and you will let me fuck you every morning before I leave the house, is that the plan, Paul? Paul replied, yes, why not.

Paul, that's absurd dude; Read my lips, I love Daniel and that won't change. Paul said, now you're double talking; that's not what you said while we were fucking, you fucked me like a man in love.

Axel respond, Paul don't fuck this up, we will always be family and that's enough. Do you understand Paul; I need you to be loyal to me, always; Paul answered, you got it boss.

(We must respect Daniel, with no reservations; Daniel is mature enough, he's my equal; he's my first love and I'm his; He's my journey and that won't change.)

Paul asked does that mean we're not going to get together again. Axel said, I'm not sure so you stay on standby, I might need you to help me relieve stress. Paul respond, okay, but to be clear, you want me to hang around in case you need to fuck me? Axel respond, is there a problem? Paul answered no dude, it's all about you; Paul it's not a big deal, don't complicate it.

Paul Let's go dude, we'll get something from the restaurant to go, it's late I must go home.

Please remember, Daniel is way more important than what we did; It was just sex, no exception, squash any emotions you might have for me, I'm not available, (Don't feel rejected we're family.) Oh yeah, limit your Conversation when talking to me at the party it's for the best.

Paul and I are connected forever, we'll always have a close friendly relationship, perhaps we'll fuck from time to time.

He opened up to me about his feelings; He explained, he has always had an attraction for the same sex, he said he just hasn't ever acted on it, until I came into the picture. He went on saying, when he notices Daniel and I spending time together, said he wasn't prepared to find out about his brother, he was totally surprised.

Paul went on saying, he spends time at bookstores trying to find information on the gay lifestyle. He's also concerned about what his future looks like. Paul and his dad, Mr. Bernal are License Electricity Technicians, they have a business together, their business comes from local Utility Companies, and Government contracts, very lucrative. He told me he has $100,000 in his savings account, and he's prepared to go out on his own. He said, it is clear to him, he knew right away what was going on with Daniel and me, he said I had no idea Daniel could be interested in the same sex, he can't understand how he and his brother would have same sex interest. I told him, it's unexplainable.

I asked Paul, how does he feel personally About himself? He answered, my feelings are people should have the freedom to choose to love, based on their point of view; if it doesn't include child related, that's sexual abuse, illegal and unacceptable.

My hopes are I find someone like you. Paul, there is only one of me, but I am sure you will find someone you can love and be happy with.

Axel deciding to seek help for what he thinks is a sex addiction. "I have had many offers for sex with some of Daniel's mates, I gave in a couple of times, I couldn't help it because they desired my dick and wanted to experience being fucked in the ass." Axel does not mention it to Daniel because he wants to always have someone on standby to fuck, outside of he and Daniel's relationship.

Here's the thing, what these dudes want the most is for Axel to put his dick in their ass, but all of them says, "I'm not gay, but I'll do whatever you want me to do."

Daniel and Paul have a close relationship, there tight, they are a close family; it just that like most families, some things are just not talked about. That's where the phrase come from; "I'm coming out," literally.

As for Daniel, he still doesn't have a clue about his brother, that means It'll be my job to enlighten him, what he can't ever know is that Paul and I are a lot closer than he's aware.

Axel sometimes wonders if Daniel has a sexual desire for anyone else other than him; his thoughts are, being a man and he's clearly into men on men, he must see someone he could be interested in, or is it just my way of thinking?

"Gaping Jaw"

Chapter IV

Ms. Kingston has everything ready for Raymond's sendoff party, Raymond and Axel is excited; Raymond said, Axel by the way, I like your new cut, it's a fresh look dude, I know your boyfriends loves it, Axel said, yeah right dude. Raymond is also excited about going to New York, he takes a one-way flight to New York City, he will stay for one year. The back lawn is all set up. Axle and Daniel called all their friends; the party starts at 7pm.

Thirty five of Raymond's and Axel's friends showed up, including Katy, and Jamal, Axel invited them; he thought that would distract Daniel, his chance is greater, to get to Jamal, It crossed Axel's mind again to have sex with Jamal, he spoke with Jamal and ask him would he like to go to his room to look around. "It's okay, we will not stay long I don't want to be missed."

Jamal followed Axel to his room, as soon as they entered, Axel said to Jamal, you like me? Jamal said, yes dude; if I am not mistaken you want to have sex with me, right? Jamal said yes, Axel asked could I penetrate your ass, this is just casual mutual sex, nothing serious? Jamal answered, I understand but not here, I will pick you up early tomorrow morning you can visit me at my home, no one will be there.

Axel kissed him, and asked, is this your first time? Jamal answered yes. Axel told Jamal Daniel and I are a couple; I am sure you guessed that already? Jamal said yes, Axel said you know what condoms are? he said yea, my parents always make sure I have some at my disposal. Axel said awesome, done deal! Jamal said, dude your hair looks fucking good, did you do it for me? Axel said yeah dude, thanks for that.

Daniel has his mind set on having sex with Katy, everyone was socializing, getting to know each other. They took advantage of that thinking they would not be noticed, Daniel and Katy talked about having sex again because Katy is taking a daily contraceptive. Daniel told her he is only available for agreed mutual sex, secretly. Daniel asked, can I call you tomorrow morning? She said yes, I'll wait for your call. (Daniel was excited,) his eyes peering around at the crowd, quickly kissed Katy on her cheek, and said "I missed you;" see you tomorrow; he looked around again and noticed Axel and Jamal walking from the house, he thought to himself, Axel is a fucking bitch, I can't leave him along for a moment; Jamal fucking wants my boyfriend. Katy watch Daniel as he walked away, thinking to herself, I'm going to seriously fuck him. Katy is a 5"11, brown skinned, brown eyes, sister; she weighs 125lbs, with a big curly Afro.

Ms. Kingston were impressed with the crowd she thought they looked like young business men and women; their all are well dressed. She spoke with each student she met complementing them, the party when well as expected. "These are good young men and women I know they had an enjoyable time."

Raymond gave a speech about his going away to New York and when he was expected to return, I were so proud of him! He sang a beautiful song to Axel; it touch Axel so much he cried. (Raymond named the song.) "unfold Your Wings and fly higher."

The next day Axel anxiously called Jamal early morning, Jamal answered at once, he has a private phone in his room. Axel asked, are you ready, Jamal said I'll leave now. Axel asked are you sure it's okay, we can put it off for another day? Jamal answered, for sure dude it's not a problem; Axel said yay! See you soon.

Axel Big Whiteish cock got hard just talking about it, thought to himself, I'm always horny I guess it's because I'm a young man; Daniel is always horny too, that's why we have so much sex. Maybe when we get older, not so much, or he somehow finds out about my infidelity behavior, promiscuous doesn't feel like I'm cheating on Daniel, it feels like muy curioso.

Jamal arrived, I waited for him at the end of my driveway, I get into his car, I said, hey Jamal, he said hey dude I'm so glad you call. Dude, you look so different. Axel response with a reserved look and said, yay!

let's talk before we get to your home but keep driving. Jamal, you stayed in my mind after you, Fabian, Daniel, and I were at McDonald's. If we do this you cannot tell anyone, Especially Daniel.

Jamal asked, is this a one-time thing, Axel said that's up to you, it depends on how things works out after this time.

Daniel and I made a promise we will never have sex with any other than with each other, do you understand? Jamal replied, Yeah dude, I understand.

Axel said, I'll call when it's possible for me, why didn't you say how you felt when I was tutoring you, we could have gotten together a while ago? Axel, I was afraid, not sure how I should approach you. Axel said, I invited you to McDonald's so we all could get to know each other, but you surprised me by flirting with me, you made my cock hard. Jamal said, thanks for the invite, I came because I wanted to see you, he went on saying, I hoped you would respond that way, I was erect as well. Jamal asked Axel, do you think you're sexy Axel? Axel answered, absolutely not; I can't see why people make such a big deal over me; I see myself to be just like everyone else. Jamal asked, do you like all the attention you' are getting? Axel said, fuck no. It gets in the way of me just being sociable; Jamal said, you do realize you're fucking off on your best mate. Axel said, don't remind me.

I'm just Axel, with a big whitish dick, I'm going to put in your ass and make you cum, that's what you want, right? Jamal answered, that's exactly what I want. Axel said, good deal.

Jamal your home is beautiful and large, do you get lonely sometimes? thanks dude, yeah, sometimes, I hoped to meet someone like you one day; let's go in, we'll go upstairs to my room, thanks Jamal. No problem, do you want a beer? I'm good. Jamal let's do this now. We're heading toward his room; I'm walking behind him close enough to touch his ass; I asked Jamal again are you sure. Jamal replied, yeah dude, no worries.

Jamal said, let's get naked, and get a condom when you're ready, I said okay. It's obvious Jamal wants me to fuck him, this is how it always happens, it's like their all talking to each other, saying Axel has the best dick in town, it also funny it's always dude's that wants me the most. The females looks at me too with the come fuck me look on their faces, but I think their afraid to approach me in that way, so I always kiss and hug them because I only see them as my girlfriends.

Jamal and I are erect, pointed towards each other, I say Jamal your cock is fat and long, he asked, you're afraid? I said, of course not.

I started by kissing him powerfully, intensifying. I said, Jamal you're fucking hot, kneel, put my dick in your mouth and keep sucking until I stop you, Jerk yourself off while sucking, that turns me on.

Jamal sucking with his juicy hot mouth, his breath is warn breathing on my dick, I'm holding back my cum, trying not to explode in his mouth.

Jamal said to Axel your dick is pretty and long, Axel said and whiteish, you like? Yeah, dude I fucking love you, Axel immediately paused and said what you say? Jamal answered, no dude I meant I love it.

Axel said keep sucking, it feels so good, Jamal paused and asked, am I better than Daniel, Axel said don't talk, concentrate on sucking my dick. Axel said, lie on your stomach Jamal I want to put my whiteish dick in your ass hole, do you have lube? Jamal answered, yes it's on the table, Jamal roll over so I can see you ass hole, I'm going to rub you down to make you more comfortable.

(The thought came to Axel's mind, thinking he want to lick Jamal's ass hole, but he didn't this time, because he wanted to reserve that for Daniel only.)

Jamal quickly rolled over onto his stomach. Axel put on a condom, and then he penetrate Jamal with his finger slowly, rubbing lotion between his legs, massaging his buttocks and nuts, reaching the back end of his dick; then went into Jamal ass, saying fuck this dick Jamal; Jamal started moaning, saying don't stop it feels so good dude.

Axel fucking forcefully for a long time, jumping up and down in Jamal's ass, than he said, Jamal I'm fucking Cumming dude, Jamal said keep fucking I'm Cumming too, Axel said, I'm Cumming in my condom, can you feel it? Jamal said fucking yes dude. Axel said, you are awesome Jamal, you're killing my dick. Axel collapse on Jamal's back side, saying, I'm still Cumming, push your ass back on my dick faster. Jamal said get up dude, Axel said you want more? Jamal Rolling over to lying on his back, Axel started giving Jamal head, Jamal moaning more, and louder, Axel, at the heat of the moment, he start licking Jamal's ass hole, Jamal said, fuck dude you are going to make me cum again.

Axel said not so loud Jamal, Axel putting his throbbing whiteish dick back into his ass hole, Jamal jerking off desperately. He cries out I'm Cumming dude, shooting his cum in my face and mouth, his cum is warm and sweet, I said, fucking awesome Jamal, I'm I doing it right? Jamal replied, I feel so good dude, you're fantastic.

Jamal relaxed, Axel asked, are you okay. Jamal answered fucking yes dude. Axel asked do you want more Jamal? Jamal answered no I'm fucking good dude; Axel, I should take you home now but let's take a quick shower; Okay Jamal, you're the boss.

While in the shower, Axel kissing all over Jamal, kissing up and down his back and his ass, their boners pointed outward, He said, Jamal I'm going to put my boner in your ass, Axel got a fresh condom and quickly put it on. Jamal said, go for it dude, Axel put his hard boner in Jamal's wet ass, Jamal bent downward, Axel fucking him so hard Jamal said dude I'm fucking Cumming, fuck me harder dude. Axel fucking Jamal expeditiously, and pull out fast, ejaculated on Jamal ass, holding him tightly, Jamal turned around, kissing Axel, he said dude that was so good, we must go now, (I'll be here whenever you need me, Just call me dude, I'm your soldier). Axel said indeed you are.

After Jamal drove Axel home, Axel told Jamal remember I'll call you when it's possible to get together again. Yep, dude I'll see you later. Axel said, I'm trusting you, for my sake don't fuck up. Jamal said bye dude, one day you'll belong to me. Axel laughed walking off, Jamal said wait dude, I almost forgot to tell you my parents said I could have a after graduation party at our home, she said I could invite fifty of our friends, parents are welcomed too, everyone must wear suits and cocktail dresses. I'm so excited, I'm going to get with you, and we will put together an invitation list. Axel replied, awesome dude, we will start planning ASAP, we are going to work well together.

As soon as I got into my house my mother asked, are you going with me to take your brother to the airport? I said yes, mom give me a second, I'm going to the restroom to wash up, where have you been Axel, jogging mom. Raymond said, yeah right Axel, you better stay out of trouble while I'm away, I love you Axel. Ditto, dude I'm going to miss you. Mom said let's go we must be on time. We all got in the SUV like a perfectly ordinary family.

The same morning Katy and Daniel talked over the phone, Daniel asked, can I come over now? of course Daniel, hurry, but we have time. Okay, Daniel thought to himself, while driving to Katy's home. (What am I doing.) He feels he's doing something wrong; it feels like he's disloyal to Axel, but he's heading her way anyways.

He arrived, kiss Katy as he walks in, she smile and said, I missed being alone with you, did you miss me? Daniel replied, Yup, are you really okay with us getting together just for sex? Katy said yes, you think girls don't get horny; we do, and I chose you to be the fuck boy-toy today, are you okay with? Daniel said yes. Katy said, and I have a condom for you; Katy asked, have you ever used one before? Daniel answered, yes, Katy asked with whom, Daniel answered, we will talk about that later, are you with someone Daniel, no. What about Axel, is he seeing someone? I didn't come to talk about Axel, Katy said, oh no worries, she said I have not been with anyone but you. Daniel asked, why do you have condoms, Katy answered, I am seeing someone we have not had sex we're still getting to know one another, I'm sure I will, he's a lovely man but we're not committed. Daniel said really; you know we don't have to do this, right? Katy said Yes, I want to fuck you unless you feel you are being unfaithful to someone? No, I'm good I want to be with you, we have unfinished business.

(Daniel thinking to himself this doesn't change have I feel about Axel.)

Katy and I undresses and begin kissing, I start to feel more comfortable; She ask me to give her some head and I had no idea how to do that, but I begin licking her pussy and she start to cum immediately, screams in excitement, my dick felt like it was going to explode, she scream, my fucking pussy is so fucking hot Daniel, put your big dick in my pussy, make sure your condom is tight and fuck my ass hole too, fuck me good, Daniel fucking her like he's an animal, switching from her pussy to her ass hole, saying you are amazing Katy!

(Daniel pensó para sí mismo, sabía que me había faltado coño.)

We fucked for about an hour I came twice, Katy came six time and I felt it each time, she's fucking awesome!

When we were done, Katy said hanging out with Axel, this what you are missing. He said I must go, trying to avoid talking about Axel.

I'll call you when I'm free again, Katy why are you so curious about Axel and me? She asked, is that a problem Daniel, are you hiding something from me? No, maybe we can have lunch soon and I'll share with you what's up with us.

Katy answered, okay and remember you don't have to be shame I'm your best girlfriend, you can be opened and honest with me.

Daniel went to the bathroom to clean himself up, rushed to his car, thinking, I must tell Axel because if he finds out he will say I am a trader, it could be over for us.

The next day I picked Axel up has usual we were heading to school, it seem since I met Axel my days are full, we both always have things to do throughout our day, But we manage to still spend time together. I said to Axel good morning, I missed you yesterday, so did I Daniel.

What did you do after the party at my home. I went home and slept until the next day, oh, what about Sunday? That's what I want to talk to you about.

Can we meet after school, Axel said, I'm sure I can squeeze you in, what time works best for you Daniel? after school, I will get done with practice early, we'll go to have hamburgers. Okay, Daniel I'll ride the bus after school Downtown, I'll see you there. Are you okay, Daniel answered yes, I'm fine, just feels like I need to be honest with you.

You're right Daniel be honest, we will fix it, no worries. I jumped out of the car walking towards my building I run into Jamal, he saw me getting out of Daniel's car, waving to Daniel. Axel told Jamal, walk with me; Jamal said how can I help you today? Axel replied, a deepthroat blowjob and a black cup of jo.

Daniel said he and I need to talk after school; Jamal asked does he know? I answered, I Think it's about him; I'm not sure, no worries for you, just remember you're my soldier, loyalty is especially important. No problem dude, when we go to college my studies are math, business management so, I'll help you for practice, you are doing a lot here at school I'll be your assistant, that the least I can do. Axel said, Jamal you don't owe me anything, you're one of my besties. Axel went on saying, I'm working to get college credits, I have already completed high school. Dude you're going to be a lawyer, right? Axel answered, for sure, and I'm going to keep your ass out of jail; they went to class and the day went by fast to them because they have so much going on, all of them.

Axel is at the hamburger joint, sitting at a table, a tall dude standing over him, they are laughing and talking, Axel was telling the dude, I see you checking me out, what's with that, he smile; Daniel showed up, the young man walked off. Daniel said, Hi Axel thanks for meeting me, who is your friend? Axel answered, Just a dude that works here, I don't know him. Daniel said no problem. Axel I hope we could work this situation out.

Explain, you have my attention. Axel, please forgive me, I will get straight to the point, I slept with Katy Sunday morning, I didn't know how to be honest at the time when you asked me what I did Sunday.

She and I spoke at the party and agreed to have sex again; I did it because she was more prepared this time, I went to her home, and we had mad sex, It felt fucking awesome dude. Axel asked, do you feel bad about it and why? I feel I betrayed you because of what we agreed to. Daniel asked, you okay with it? Axel said yes because I had sex with Jamal the same day you was with Katy; I called Jamal and asked could I come visit; Daniel said I don't understand, is it over for us? Yes, if that's what you need in your life, What I mean is we can learn from this, or it could be over if you think it's best; It's obvious our relationship is vulnerable.

Daniel respond, No I want us to stay together, I told Katy it's just sex, it won't happen again, she agreed; I think I'm going to tell her you're my boyfriend. Axel said, hold on dude! Are you're sure we're ready for that? Daniel respond, yeah, I want to be free so I can focus on you without any guilt. I love you and I hope you still love me. Axel said, Daniel I love you forever and nothing can change that. I'm sorry I slept with Jamal; It was all my fault, I kissed him at the party and told him I wanted to fuck him just for sex, he was okay with that.

Daniel asked, I'm still the only guy you're interested in, have you fucked anyone else, are you in love with Jamal or anyone else other than me? did you let him penetrate you? Hold up dude, that's too many questions at once. But to answer your questions, No, no and no.

(Axel just lied, he has had sex with two other guys besides Daniel and Paul.)

Axel said, I can love only one person at a time and at this time you're my journey. We need to recommit to each other and go from there. I have an idea; I have been seeking help for my continuous urge for sex; These tendencies could get me, or us in trouble. I have sexual desire for other guys and it's a great possibility I'm going to act on my infatuations. There is a gay group that helps guys like me, the group leader told me it's a smart move, and by the way he's my assist coach. What do you think? Daniel asked, I am not enough for you? Yes you are, I love you with my whole heart, if we're going to be happy we just need to put work in to help me out. That's what love is.

Axel asked, you still think you can love me? Daniel said, I need you, you are my partner forever; we have a plan. Daniel, I don't want you to get hurt in this relationship with. I'm sure I will get better now that you know, it's your move.

Axel just tell me what you need me to do? Axel said, exactly what you are doing now, be supportive. Axel, I'm going to take care of you, don't worry. Thanks Daniel, I love you as well.

Axel asked, do you think you can be faithful, you fucked up too? Daniel said, yes, we have much to look forward to, we can put this behind us.

But how will you avoid Jamal? Axel said, I don't have to avoid him we have an understanding, he's going to work for me as my personal assistant; he offer, I accepted his offer, once we're in college he'll be helpful. He decided to go to SMU, I told him wise choice. Axel Did you enjoy fucking him? Yes he's incredibly good in bed, he let me man handle his ass hole, we're not in love, that's the difference.

I'm more concerned about Katy because I think Katy wants you back. Oh, Jamal and I used condoms, I'm sure we are okay, and everyone that's involved, we all should always practice protective sex, safer sex. Daniel said, Katy and I used condoms as well. Axel respond, than we all on the same page.

Daniel I missed you; I want to make love to you when can we get together again? Daniel said, I will call you later this evening, I missed you too, please Axel I love you, please don't fuck up again. Axel said, You can count on me, and once I get the help I need we'll be just fine.

They were at their homes for an hour, Daniel called Axel, can you come to my home now? Axel answered? Yes wait for me at your back door. Daniel said, Will do boss.

Axel knock once and Daniel said we have two hours, wearing nothing, his dick looking at me, big and stiff. Daniel said take your clothes off, I did very fast, Daniel pulled me by the hand, we went in his room. He immediately start sucking my dick, saying this what you going to miss if you fuck up anymore. Daniel continues sucking, drooling on my dick, I were moaning loudly. Daniel got up from the floor, kissing me. He guided me to his bed and said, I'm going to fuck you, I have condoms, he put on a condom.

Axel said I'm here to please you! I laid on my stomach, I put lube in my ass, he begins fucking me very slowly, Daniel said it feels so good inside you, are you okay.

Axel said yes, I'm fucking good! Daniel said I'm going to lie on my back, I want you to sit on my dick and roll your ass around with my dick inside you, okay, Daniel begin fucking me so good, I begin jerking my dick while he's fucking and suddenly I shot cum all over Daniel's face, we were panting loudly, Daniel came out of me and said put my dick in your mouth, suck me until I cum, I gave Daniel the best head job ever, trying to show him he's satisfying to me, so he want feel insecure. When we were done, Daniel and I kissed for a long time and axel said I must go, Daniel remember you're my love forever no matter what happens between us I will always love you.

Daniel preguntó ¿le dijiste a Jamal sobre nosotros? Axel respondió, sí. Daniel dijo entonces que no espero que se cruce conmigo, ¿verdad? No, él está en mi equipo pase lo que pase, es leal. Nos vemos mañana. Daniel dijo te amo Axel, soy más leal que Jamal, dijo Axel a tu manera. Daniel, Dejarme a Jamal, es mi soldado. Daniel responde, no rompas mi corazón amigo.

(Daniel asked, did you tell Jamal about us? Axel replied, yes. Daniel then said that I don't expect him to cross paths with me, should I? No, he's on my team no matter what, he's loyal. See you tomorrow. Daniel said I love you Axel, I'm more loyal than Jamal, Axel said in your own way, Daniel Leave Jamal to me, he's my soldier. Daniel respond, don't break my heart my friend.)

"No More Hiding"

Chapter V

This is where life begins as a gay young man outed himself, deciding to live free and out of the closet. I asked my mom; may I talk to you? She replied, yes anytime.

Mom I'm gay. I grappled with the thought in my mind before I came to this conclusion, it's clear to me, It feels normal to Daniel and I. For me I was like a dragon flower waiting to bloom; I was not coerced, guided, or taking advantage of. Daniel and I decided we want to live as a same sex couple. Please forgive me for not talking to you first but Didn't think I needed to because you and the rest of the family didn't seem to care, it wasn't a problem for you all; I'm still the boy you raised, I'm a respectful person to all people, the people at my school has much respect for me and have been supportive.

We are not out totally as a couple because only a very few people are in the loop. My mom said, thinks Axel for being honest with me, you're right I have always thought you might be but please remember we care about you and what kind of person you are; I just want you and Raymond to be happy. Just because I thought you could be gay is not enough for me to conclude without talking to you directly about your sexual preferences, I thought you'll come to me when you're ready, respectfully I was waiting for you, I know you are an honest person, and wouldn't live a lie.

Mom, I'm in a sexuality group, we talk about how to be responsible, the group leader is my assist coach, this is what we do outside of the school, all voluntarily, to any one that wants to come, we only share our experience, strength, and hope. We meet for an hour a day, early mornings before school, it's been informative.

We get to meet other people that has the same interest, no one is forced to talk or do anything that their uncomfortable with. The coach has a boyfriend that's a Doctor at Parkland Hospital, he said they have been together for 12 years. Axel have you told your brother? No, I just assumed he already knew, it came up in our conversation before, but I'll make it clear. He's my first friend and he knows me; I think better than anyone.

Mother you all has always made me feel like I'm free to be myself and I never had to explain about who I am. Mom said, we all love you for who you are, as always.

Has Daniel told his family? No ma'am. Ms. Kingston said, I really would feel much better if you and Daniel would tell his family, It's important that they know as well, keeping secrets are unhealthy.

Axel do you and Daniel need an evaluation? No mom. I'm going to get an appointment for you to get your annual physical and blood tests as well. Okay mom thanks: Daniel and I will tell his parents ASAP, thanks mom for being so accepting and understanding. It might be uncomfortable for you to hear this but I'm not a virgin anymore, Daniel and I are having sex, safe sex of course. Axel's mom said, good to know, but you're still going to get a blood test; you're okay with it? Also, you should encourage Daniel to get tested too. Yes ma'am, I will talk to Daniel ASAP. Thanks mom.

Ms. Kingston asked, Is Daniel your only boyfriend? Yes, per say, but there are other guys expresses interest in me, but we all are just friends and most of the guys and girls I tutored. She asked, Do you all do drugs? No mom, we are all drug free.

Oh, by the way mom, maybe you and my dad should talk about me getting a new car? We'll see Axel, your dad is doing much better now. Axel said, good mom, it's over for you and him, yes or no?

yes. Your dad has remarried, he has a new wife her name is Liz . Wait, Wow! He's going to wire me twenty thousand dollars tomorrow; he lives in Atlanta with his new wife. Wow, really? Yes and this money is to help you and Raymond while you all are in school. Axel said, this is exciting news Mom! Why didn't you tell me? I was waiting for the right time.

Axel called Raymond in New York and said what's up bruh? Raymond answered, how are you pretty boy? Raymond if you don't mind, I'm a pretty man now. Oh, excuse me are you pregnant yet? Axel said, fuck dude, you are insane. They laughed and went on talking.

Raymond asked are you out of the closet Axel? And don't say you're not gay. I have always known; you are my gay brother; I will always love you. Are you still fucking Daniel? Yes, he's my boyfriend. But Raymond it would have been nice if you would have walked me to the closet door, metaphorically speaking. Raymond respond, yeah, it's a new thing for me as well; I knew you would figure things out. Axel said, no worries, I'm good. Raymond asked, so you're sure you're gay or you are just enjoying having a gay experience and it'll pass over time? No dude, I am gay.

Raymond did you find a girlfriend? Yes and she's going to come to Dallas with, she's my promoter. Axel are you glad about dad coming home? Axel answered, Yes, are you? For sure, I missed him.

Raymond, I'm attending a gay group because I'm having a problem with my desires for other guys, I'm not doing anything to cause more attention to myself, but they seem to have fervent desire for me. The person I more concerned about is Daniel's brother, he's in to me as well. Raymond asked, he's gay? Well, Raymond he isn't sure, he just know he wants me. Raymond asked, Have you fucked him? Sadly, I have.

Fucking awesome dude, Does Daniel know? No, and Paul threaten to tell him, if I don't break up with Daniel, but I don't think he'll go to that extreme, he thinks he's in love with me. Axel be careful with him because you don't know what he's capable of doing. Maybe you should tell Daniel? Axel replied, fuck no dude; that would be the end of our relationship, that's why I'm in the group to learn from other people that's gay. Raymond asked, are there girls in the group? Yes, and most of them are gay as well. Oh yeah Raymond after the graduation ceremony, My Friend is having a big party at his house; His mom is going to have it catered. You and your girlfriend are invited as well. Okay Axel, I will be home in two months. Raymond said tell Paul we need to talk as soon as I return from New York. Axel said, will do, but he's a nice dude and we are friends so no worries, okay Raymond? Okay dude, I have to go, I see you in approximately 12 weeks. Okay Dude take care. Axel remember to practice safer sex, and you don't have to have sex because someone desires you, you have to be careful, I must go now, Peace out bruh.

Paul is a very good-looking man; he is secretly struggling with the fact that he has an attraction for Axel. He's aware, he and Axel will never have a committed relationship, but he's more concerned about how will he satisfy his desire for the same sex. Paul and Daniel were seeing girls before Axel came into the picture, same sex never crossed Daniel's mind; Daniel were around many guys alone and exposed and never got sexually stimulated. Paul wrestle with the thought, "I'm I gay, or will this feeling pass over time."

I called Daniel after I spoke with my sponsor, Daniel joined me a few times just to see what goes on in our meetings, he even had a sponsor. He answered my call; Hi Axel, What are you doing, did you talk with your sponsor? Axel answered, Yes I did, he didn't have much to say, I told him I'll need more time to know how I'm doing. Axel I won't be attending the group anymore. Axel asked, when did you make that decision without me? I didn't need your approval, so that's why I didn't mention it, It doesn't matter when I decided to not attend the group but, I think you should just deal with your own situation, I'm committed to you, you are the one with the problem. Axel's response, OK Daniel whatever you think is best for us.

Daniel, I told my mom I'm gay. Dude, what did she say? She asked me are you my boyfriend? I said yes. Axel, I'm fucking in love with you, we're free to love more openly!

Daniel, I also told Raymond; Dude, you are awesome, are they okay with? Axel said, Yes, they are glad I came out to them. Daniel asked are you happy you did, Axel said yea. Daniel said, Axel all we have to do is be patient and we will be able to go forward with our plans. I love you and I want things to work out for us.

I'm home alone would you like to come over to visit? No, I don't want Paul to interrupt us and what about your parents? My parents went out for dinner and cocktails, they will be out late tonight, If Paul comes home no big deal. Axel I know Paul has feelings for you and I figured If he see us together it'll help him to get over you; Axel replied, wait for me at the door. I arrived Daniel said, Let's go to the bedroom; Daniel are you sure? Yes. We were in his room for a while only kissing and bonding, Daniel whispering in my ear, Axel you make me feel so good, your fore play is very passionate, please never stop loving me this way, you make me feel whole; he went on saying, Axel I know you want to fuck me, but I think we should wait until after graduation, it's too soon, you're still sanctioned, I see you have a boner; I will only jerk you off.

Axel said I'll take what I can get. Axel asked, I want to give you a blow job and jerk myself off, are you cool with? He kissed me and said I'm all yours.

I kneel and begin pleasuring him, he taste so good it was hard not to release. He said put my balls in your mouth, I did what he asked, kept sucking, licking, and drooling, causing his dick to be extremely wet and hard, while jerking myself off. Daniel, running his fingers through my hair, pushing his cock in and out of my wet hot mouth. Axel I really like your shoulder length blonde hair! you look more like an Albano It's like being with a whole new person; Axel asked, Daniel are we going to talk, I can't suck you off if we're talking; Daniel replied, don't stop, it feels so good, he asked where do you want me to shoot my load? I stood up and said ejaculate on my hard boner! We came the same time shooting on each other's boner. We kissed and I kneeled again continue sucking Daniel hard wet boner, he asked, can I ejaculate in your mouth? I said why not, I love you and everything about you.

I continued sucking and licking, he shot in my mouth, Daniel said, swallow dude; I did his cum is warm, it felt like love going down my throat, when Daniel and I have sex we don't hold back, we give each other what we need. I asked Daniel, can I penetrate your ass, I won't take long. Daniel pulled his pants off and told me to put lubricant in his ass. I did and put on a condom, went into him slowly, Daniel said, go for it Axel. I started to jump up and down into his ass so deep he started saying oh I'm so horny fuck me good Axel. I pulled out, I yanked my condom off and shot my big heavy load all over Daniel's back, I screamed, saying, fuck dude, you're killing me, stroking my dick, hitting Daniel's ass with my dick, then I relaxed on his back side and almost went to sleep.

Daniel said Axel we should get up. Axel said, right, may I use the restroom. Daniel said of course. I came out after cleaning myself up, went back into Daniel's room he said come lie with me for a few minutes, He was still naked, I started kissing his nipples, he were getting a stiff Boner again. He guided my head down towards his hard boner, I opened my mouth and began licking and sucking him immediately he jerked himself, ejaculated, trembling, his eyes were watery. I was kissing his face and putting my tongue in and out of his mouth, saying I love you dude, we are going to be together forever, our future looks bright. Do you want me to stay longer? Daniel answered, no, I'm sure you have a lot to do but, thanks for coming by.

I got up walking toward the door, Daniel said, wait Axel, he kissed me and said, I'll see you tomorrow morning. Okay I love you dude.

Axel made it home and went to take a shower, while in the shower he thought about Paul, instantly his dick start to throbbing, and he couldn't resist the urge to jerk off.

"but I didn't because I want to stop entertaining the idea of fucking Paul again."

The next day I went to the meeting, once I were in the room everyone greeted and sat down, the coach said hello everyone; let's get started. First is anyone late for school or work because you're coming to this meeting? Everyone said no. He went on to say, okay, let's talk.

We're going to stand, briefly talk about what's going on in our lives and it don't have to be about your sexual relationships, just whatever you feel comfortable with. However, do reach out to your sponsor to have a more private talk.

I stood up and said, I'm Axel, happy to be here, I just wanted to say Daniel and I are doing better as a couple, but I still have much work to do to better understand myself and how I can and will change my behavior.

I understand boys will be boys, but what I want for my boyfriend is to give him my undivided attention, not just when we are having sex.

Coach said, thanks Axel; is there anyone like to respond to Axel's comment.

A guy stood up and said my name is Benjamin and I am a top, bottom. Axel, your boyfriend is fucking hot dude; However, I feel you and Daniel should give it more time, you are already on the right road by coming here. Oh, by the way Axel I like your fresh look, you're fucking hot dude, very good looking. Axel said thanks dude, nice to know you, maybe we can talk sometime? Benjamin respond, cool.

The Coach said okay guys we don't have much time, Please go straight to school and to work after you leave here. And don't be late. Is there anyone else need to share? A young man from a different school stood up and asked Axel, I'm Vince, are you and your boyfriend having sex, if so with condoms? Axel answered, yes, and yes. Vince said thanks for being honest maybe we can hang sometimes? Axel said, maybe. The Coach said, no fraternizing while we are meeting; take it home. Okay guys, condoms are essential. Let's end the meeting.

(We will end the meeting with this note, remember to treat others the way you want to be treated. Be responsible people.)

Make it a wonderful day guys, thanks for coming.

Axel went to school by bus and as soon as he arrived; Daniel were waiting for Axel at the front of Axel's building; he said, hi dude, how did the meeting go? Axel answered, as well as expected. Daniel said I'm glad you are staying with the group, it's good for us. I love you and no one else is more interesting to me then you are, I'll never give in to sexual fantasies every time I get a boner, this's what I need from you is loyalty, exactly what you require of me. Axel you said what I want is as important as what you want, right? Yes dude, of course.

Well, what I want is for us to do what we planned, go to college, and make a future together. When I met you I thought I were straight, now because of you I'm sure who I am and what I want; Not to alarm, but I think if it doesn't work out for us I'll probably be with some other guy. Axel please don't put me in that position because there are other guys showing interest in me. Okay Daniel, but do you already have someone in mind? No. But it's possible. So, you are saying there isn't any guy you could be interested in, just for fucking? Daniel said. No, not at this point. We are still learning as we go, Just be faithful and trust the process.

(Let's go to class, I'll see you after school).

Axel has Jamal's visitation list; they formed a graduation committee of 12 young men and women that will decide who's in and who's not. The objective is to put all the graduation events together and get the visitations mailed out. Everything must be ready in two months.

Axel added Paul to the list with one guest allowed. He wants Paul to be there so they can end what Paul think they had together; His plans are to introduce Paul to Jamal hoping they will hit it off.

Axel is happy to move on from High School to College and into his apartment. He did talk with Jamal about living with him, like Axel expected he said he can't because he plans to transfer, so he can work while in school, he's moving to Las Vegas to work as a Banker unless he gets a more attractive offer, here in Dallas.

Daniel decided for us to live together, and he's going to pay the household bills; he won't have a job, but he gets a monthly allowance and he insist we do things this way.

I'll start working at a Law Firm as an office manager; I only have a month after graduation to prepare for work, I will be making enough money to live alone but, we'll do it Daniel's way.

Paul called me to asked if there was a mistake made, he said I graduated two years ago; I got a card in the mail saying I'm invited to a party, rsvp you for more details? It's not a mistake Paul, I added you to the guest list, I hope you don't mind, you're my friend. Paul respond, No problem I can come if you want me to come. Axel said, yes I want you to be there so you can meet the host. His Name is Jamal, Do you know him? No Axel. Well, Paul, he's a nice guy and I feel you and him might have things in common. Paul asked and what is that Axel? Are you trying to push me off to someone else other than you. Yes, I don't want you to expect us to be together, what happened between us was awesome, but it could never happen again, it's our secret for life; Daniel and I will never break up, and I want you to accept that.

You like guys so, have an open mind and be extra kind to Jamal, you never know what could happen. Axel I haven't been with a guy except for you, I'm into you, I am not sure if I'll like other guys the same; I'm not gay, just only for you. Axel said and that's what has to change. Please do it for me? You can still bring one guest with you, are not. Axel, are you sure you don't won't to be with me, I know you have feelings for me? Yes I'm sure, I have to be honest; I really like you and if it weren't Daniel it would be you. But we'll be good friends, and we can all hang out together, but Daniel deserves respect. Sounds good Axel, I'll talk to you later. Thanks for taking my call. No problem Paul, Please remember to wear a suit to the party. No problem, I want to look good for you. No dude, you'll look good for Jamal. "Oh Yeah right dude."

This is the best thing that has happened in my life, My name is Jamal Allard, I'm the only child. My last name means, "Noble Friend." All my high school friends are graduating, my besties will be here at my home for the after-graduation party. My parents are Doctors, and they are trusting me to not let things get out of control, although they will be here during the party, so will some of the other parents, the party ends at 2am, some of my mates will bring spiked punch and some of the jocks are bringing flowers from a dispensary; (But this is all on the low.)

Everyone started to arrive from out of town, Raymond and his girlfriend will stay at the Hyatt Hotel, they don't plan to stay long In Dallas, TX, they have a concert in Spain next week. My dad and his wife is here also, they will stay in the Hyatt as well. My dad and I talked, and I met his lovely wife, my mom let her boyfriend hang around, so she won't look lonely to my dad.

My dad kept his promise to my mom, and we were incredibly happy to see him again. He said to me, Axel you and your brother has really grown up, you looks so different and grown, I love your new hair style; is it true, you're gay? Yes dad I am. He said I'm so happy you came out to your family; It shows how you have grown to be a confident man.

I here you have a boyfriend, when will I meet him, Soon dad, he's excited to meet you as well. Axel dad said I'm sorry I had to leave you all. I had to get help, so I checked in a treatment center in New York, That's where I met my wife, Liz, she's a therapist, she's going to open a mental health center, with a psychiatrist in Atlanta; we're going to live in Atlanta, you know, the capital of Georgia. Yes, dad I'm aware of Atlanta, but thanks.

I also won a New York Lottery! seven hundred million dollars, but after taxes my payout is 560 million dollars. Axel respond, Wait, Dad you say I'm a millionaire? Mr. Kingston said, yes Axel we are, I am going to do everything to make it up to you all.

I here you want a new car, guess what, your new BMW will arrive tomorrow. Wait, what? You bought me a new car dad? Yes, and I'm-going to find out what Raymond wants, if he wants a new car or whatever he wants, he's my son too. Your mom did well with the both of you, I'm so proud of my family. I told your mom over the phone that I'm going to give her $20,000 but I surprised her with $20 million instead; I wired the money to her she's talking with her lawyer about the arrangements.

So, dad, to be clear I am a millionaire, right? Yes. Dad do you mind if I tell Daniel? No, he's your boyfriend, your mom told me he and his family are good people, and you trust him than it's not a problem.

I called Daniel and said I am so excited, you must come to my home now, I have something to tell you. You need to know this, and I have to tell you in person. Daniel said I'm heading your way now; I'll meet you at your patio. Are you okay? Yes Daniel, please come now!

Daniel arrived and said what's up dude? Axel kissed him and said you will need to have a seat. Daniel I'm a millionaire! My New BMW will arrive tomorrow, my Dad bought it for me. Daniel said he's in town? Yes, He's in the house now, but he's staying at the Hyatt, with his new wife. Wow Axel I would like to meet him, what do you mean you're a millionaire? My Dad won a 560-million-dollar lottery in New York. Daniel I'm going to buy us a Loft; Downtown, we won't need an apartment, I'm going to take care of us. Axel, life is going to be different; you will need to get used to having money, but I'm sure your parents will keep a close watch on you. Ideally, is to live life as normal as possible. But I'm happy, we will sit down and modify our plans. Axel said, Everything stays the same as my mom planned for me, but I'll have a car and buy my own home. You keep your place on campus and come home when it's possible, I'll drive myself to school and work; but I'm sure the first time I'll need you to help me with driving in that kind of traffic; Daniel I'm so nervous about us living together, we'll see if that works for you or just stay in the apartment together, you won't need to live on campus if you don't want to, it's totally up to you.

Daniel said, I'm nervous too, we will be fine, so busy we won't have time to be afraid, remember what you said, we are men now.

Daniel I told my mom you're going to talk to your parents about us. They will get their invitation in the mail this week, you should tell them before the party; Paul called me to make sure I meant to send him an invite. I told him we wanted him to be there, he's excited. Okay, I was only waiting until I know for sure we would be together. Axel asked, what about tonight? Daniel replied, Okay I'll do it tonight.

Daniel, do you want me to be with, when you have the talk? No, I think it's better if I do it alone. Axel said, It's all up to you; I'm only a call away. Thanks

Axel: hold on dude, also my mother wants us to get tested, ASAP. I told her we're having sex as well; Really, you weren't embarrassed to tell her that? Axel replied, No, I want us to be seen as adults.

Everyone has received their invites; we only have one week to be ready. Jamal called me and said his mom wants me to come over to go over the setup. That's when I got the chance to tell Jamal about my new car; Jamal I am getting a New Car, BMW, it'll arrive tomorrow. I'll come by as soon as I get it, tell you mom. Jamal asked, Axel how did you get a new car? My Dad is in town for the graduation and bought it for me. Wow Axel that's nice, I'm so happy for you!

Jamal you can run this by your mom. The program will include, a DJ, and my brother, Raymond and his girlfriend is going to sing and play his keyboard and between sets, he's also working on a full entertainment program, small mini bar with wine and beer for our guest, if your parents are okay with? Yes dude, totally.

Daniel is going to give a speech. We need a have finger foods and hors d'oeuvres throughout the night. We want tables in the back lawn near the pond, a car parker and two security detail.

But I'll come by as soon as I get my car. Tell her I said, thanks so much, we will use her ballroom, kitchen, and family room. Mine and Daniel parents will be there too. And tell her I want to help with the expenses. Okay Axel you call me tomorrow to keep me in the loop. No problem Jamal.

Axel at home close to the phone trying not to miss a call from anyone. Everyone is going to meet him at his home to wait for his new car to arrive. Meanwhile, Daniel is at home with his family, including Paul. He call all of them together to tell them he's gay. Daniel said to his parents, mom, dad, I'm gay and I thought It would be only fair for you to know who I am, (along with who I really am.) I love you all and very thankful to have you all as my loved ones.

Please don't think you went wrong somewhere, that's not true. I'm going to college as a proud man and that's all because of my parents. The only thing different about me is I prefer same sex relationship, which bring me to this point. I love Axel and we have been in a relationship since the day they moved into their home. We met, and it was instant chemistry. I didn't tell you all before now because I wasn't sure I wanted to be with Axel, so I waited to tell you.

(Paul looking at Daniel with a surprise look on his face, but at the same time with a proud look as if he's impressed.)

Axel and I are going to live together while in college. Axel's dad came into a lot of money he won a 560-million-dollar lottery and bought Axel a new

BMW and he is giving Axel money to buy a loft, Downtown. So, at least I have a millionaire boyfriend!

(This is all news to Paul, now he has an amazed look on his face.)

Daniel dad said, well son, mom and I had come to that conclusion, but wanted to wait, hoping you would tell us before you go to college. We love you all no matter what; Paul, did you know? Yes sir, how do you feel about this? I feel people should love who they love without outside chatter, so like you all I thought it was something he should do, come out himself.

Daniel mom said we love you and want you to be happy and if this what you want for yourself than you have our support.

I got the invite to your friends party and we're happy you all wanted us to be there, and I love getting the chance to meet Axel's parents in person and the rest of the people that means so much to you. Thank you for being honest with us. Please son don't rush in to living with Axel, maybe you should give it some time and stay in the college dorm until you're sure; you are young and could change your mind at any giving moment.

No, mom we planned it a while ago. Okay mom, I'll keep you posted. They all laugh aloud because Daniel was being funny, and she said Daniel, please keep us in the loop. Yes ma'am. Paul and his family all hugged each other and said we are family, and nothing will change that.

Daniel and Paul walked together going to Axel's home. Paul told Daniel, you know you are a lucky man, Daniel said, yes. Paul I'm aware you have feelings for Axel, Please respect us and don't be a problem for us. Paul are you gay dude? No, I'm bi-curious. (Paul said no worries you won't have any trouble out of me, thinking to himself, Axel and I will always be bonded, if I had pursued him hard enough he would be mine.)

Daniel are you and Axel going to get a place? Yes. Axel is going to buy us a home. Paul said, Wow, That's awesome dude, Axel is a millionaire? Yes. Paul said don't fuck up dude, Axel plays hard ball. Are you ready for that? Yes, I can handle my boyfriend, you just stay out of our business, if I need you I let you know. They went on to Axel's house to meet him with his family waiting for the car to arrive.

Axel introduced everyone. Axel said, dad this is Daniel and his brother, Paul. They all shook hand and hugged, and my dad said, it is nice to meet you all, we have heard so much about you. Daniel said, you as well sir.

The car arrived, everyone looking with excitement in their eyes. Axel and Daniel standing next to each other like a couple. Imagine, two 6"1 to 6'3 young men, both with the looks of model ready, their hair blowing in the air because the wind is a little high, smiling at one another.

Daniel whispered in Axel ear and said I told my parent I'm gay and we are a couple. Axel hug Daniel and said, I love you always and forever.

The red BMW arrived, it looks fabulous, four doors; Axel said, thanks mom and dad, I love it! Dad let's take a drive around the block, Axel's dad said, okay, Daniel why don't you come with us? Daniel said, yes sir! Axel's father wanted them alone with him, so he'll have the talk with them together. Daniel is a strong-willed guy, very confident, he's a stand-up kind of guy, he's a leader. Daniel thinks of himself as Axel's protector, and Axel feels the same way about Daniel.

Axel's dad looks very well, He's 6'2, his skin is pale, with shoulder length, red hair, his eyes are gray. Daniel and Mr. Kingston will get a lone very well,

Mr. Kingston is going to take Daniel under his wing because he wants smart people around him for good advice. He wants Daniel to become a business major, Life is going to be majorly different for the entire family circle, after meeting Daniel he has an Idea, he wants him to learn a managerial role of the businesses he's going to create in Dallas, he's going to open an office for Daniel and Axel to work and study while in college; It appears Mr. Kingston is being extremely generous, but on the contrary, there's a bigger picture; but it could break or make Axel and Daniel's relationship.

Axel's mom has plans of her own, she feels she has done her job as a mother, proud of her family and elated how things has turned out for her and their future. Her and Axel will have the talk after the after party at Jamal's home.

"We Are Family"

Chapter VI

Mr. Kingston said, Axel you will need to follow the rules with your beginner license, such as, you can have only one person in the car while you're driving, until you get your actual license. Your car is paid for in full, your car has an insurance policy, full coverage, but later you'll have to start your own policy and get it registered in your name, I want you to be totally independent. You should add Daniel to your policy as a driver, I'm sure there won't be any other drivers, right? No sir. Your realtor will contact you in a few days to help you find a home, or whatever type home you want, it also will be paid in full. My lawyer and I setup with our Bank a fifty million dollars trust fund for you; we will get together with our lawyers about the rest of the details. It's important that I get money distribute to my loved ones, for tax purposes, so I want to get it done quickly; I want my family to get started with their lives and finances, retain an attorney. But, one other thing you should know, you have a bank account already setup with ten million dollars, our lawyers with get with you about it as well, you have full access to it: starting now. Let stop at the park to talk for a few minutes before going back home.

Axel said, okay dad. Axel parked the car, they all got out; Axel hugged Mr. Kingston and said you are wonderful I knew you would come back to me; I love you.

Axel asked, dad are you going to set Raymond up financially? Yes, I setup a 10-million-dollar bank account for him; he has wonderful plans for his future, I want to be a part of his adult life, I love him he's a wonderful stepson. And he's loyal to us.

Axel, I wanted to tell you myself because you are my special son. Axel said, okay, whatever, but I'm a young man now; They are laughing!

Daniel, you look like a nice young man, and you are incredibly good looking, your parents did well with you, I look forward to meeting them at the party. Daniel said, thanks Mr. Kingston. Axel's dad straight forwardly asked Daniel do you like women? Daniel said yes, but I'm happier with the same sex. So, you and Axel are a couple? Yes sir, I had a girlfriend when I met Axel, I decided I rather be with him, actually we decided together. You do understand the lifestyle you all have chosen for yourselves isn't going to be easy because some people have a problem with gay folks, and you all are young and a very wealthy couple, I want you guys to be aware of who you befriend. Axel have you ever been with a girl? No dad. How do you know how you feel about a girlfriend. Dad if I wanted to be with a female I would have, but I have always had a sexual attraction for guys, if you're asking me why, I don't believe there's a why or how, Let's look at it this way, I had a choice and I chose to be with a man. I hope you are not offended; you didn't go wrong with me; I will be the best man I could be.

I'm glad you are sure what you want in life, just remember you still have much to learn, what is especially important is to get your education, so you can make good decisions. Daniel I'm sure we will get to know each other more over time because I'm never going to leave Axel alone again.

Daniel I'm sure Axel told you about our skin disorder, which is why we look so different from most people? Daniel said yes sir, Axel father asked, how do you feel about that? Daniel said, that's what attracted me to Axel, the very first time I looked into his eyes, and I was totally mesmerized, from that point we have been together; I'm in love with Axel sir.

Mr. Kingston asked, I hear you are a good football player do you plan to play professionally after college? He went on saying, Axel is going to be a wealthy Lawyer and he's going to play hard ball now, with ballers. He'll be groomed. Daniel answered, Well sir, I'm not sure yet.

You should think about it because things are going to move fast for you and Axel. I want you all to do well in school because I'm going to need smart advisors, and who's better than my son and his boyfriend; I Want you guys to be happy and the best people you can be, wealthy and smart.

Axel said, thanks dad and I won't let you down. I love you Axel and nothing will ever change that. Daniel said, Mr. Kingston thanks for accepting me as Axel's boyfriend, and most of all as a person, I will always appreciate you.

Axel dad said you're welcome, my family and I expect you to be loyal to us, right Axel? Axel respond, totally.

Okay guys we better get back before your mom start to worry about you all, and there's food at home waiting for us. Axel things will move fast, until we get everything settled, be as prepared as much as you can to keep up with what's going on, I want you to get some things taking care of before you go back to school. Okay dad thanks again. Axel dad said to Daniel, will you drive us home; Daniel said, copy that boss.

When they arrived home Axel told his dad to go on inside with the rest of them, Daniel and I need to talk briefly, we will see you all inside in a moment. Axel dad said OKAY don't be too long.

Axel and Daniel stayed in the car and when the coast was clear they kissed passionately. Axel was crying, Daniel said, I got you don't be afraid, I know this is a lot to take in and you must be overwhelmed, obviously your parents has big plans for you. Please forgive me I'm lost for words, he went on saying, what I know for sure is we love one another, and our relationship will get even stronger, and you have changed my life completely.

Axel said, I never expected for things to be this way, please tell me this is real and I'm not dreaming. Daniel kissed Axel passionately again, and said you feel real to me, this is not a dream. Are you okay now? Axel said yes, but I'm not sure I can manage all this, Daniel said I understand, neither am I, but what I do know is I'll be here with you all the way, we have your mom and dad to help us with everything. So, Axel stay strong, let's take one day at a time. Please, Axel don't do anything for me before we talk about it first? Axel said, but why? fuck dude, you're my man and I love you; you get what I want you to have, I'm rich now; You're mine, it's like we're married. Daniel said because it's not going to work that way, we are a team and a team discuss things before we act on them.

Daniel said , I want to switch my major, after speaking with your dad I can see in my future to switch to Finance, the course requirements are English, Communication, Mathematics and Accounting which means I no longer will have a scholarship.

My parents gave me a choice to not except the scholarship and I can choose a different major, because they didn't think playing football in college would be good for me, they set aside for my college intuition for five years, in case I needed another year to expand my major. Okay Daniel, but now I can help with your college funds.

Thanks Axel, we'll talk about that later, I have some other ideas I'll run them by you later, after we get settled. Axel said no problem, we can go in the house now, do I look like I've been crying? Daniel said yes, but no worries I'm sure they'll understand. Oh, by the way, your dad is awesome, and my parents is going to love him.

(Axel parents are liberals, and all the rest of the parents that's in their circle are liberal as well, their parents are in the business of public service.)

Axel and Daniel went into the house and there were more people than expected, my mom being the perfect host. Paul and Raymond are sitting together like they are enjoying each other and My dad's wife, Liz, sitting between them, with a big smile on her face. Paul Walked to Axel and Daniel and said are ya'll okay, Axel you look like you been crying?

Axel said I'm okay Paul, just give me a hug. Paul pulled axel in his arms and kissed him on each side of Axel cheek and said I love you.

Daniel said that's enough guys. Paul said you come here and let me give you a hug too, we are all family now, right Axel? Absolutely.

Ms. Kingston asked Daniel are you hungry, Daniel said yes ma'am I am. She said let's go in the kitchen I'll get you something to eat and we can talk. He said, yes ma'am, Copy that.

(Axel's Dad and Raymond sitting together talking, their smiling, Axel was pleased to see that because Raymond is especially important to Axel, and his happiness is as well.)

Raymond walked over to Axel, he said, no hemos tenido oportunidad de hablar, this is Vickie, she's from New York, we met when I first arrived there and we had some classes together, hit it off and here we are; she's my traveling companion, we'll return to New York next year. I hope I can take a vacation next year we all can vacation together. Raymond I'm going to hold you to that. Are you planning to live in New York? Raymond answered, yes, I'm going to make the announcement at the party. Axel said to Vickie, it's nice to meet you; I hope my brother is taking loving care of you, He is a wealthy man now, so don't be bashful. They laughed and she said no worries, I'm sure he'll look out for me, he's a good man as well. Axel said, you can call us anytime while ya'll are away. Okay Axel, thanks for that.

Raymond asked Axel, you like your new car? Axel said, amigo me encanta. Axel asked, Raymond, what kind of car do you have? Raymond said I don't have a car yet; I plan to buy a new car when I return from abroad.

Axel we are only going to stay until after the party, Vickie y yo temenos que tomar un vuelo. Axel said, that's fine, I'm glad you're here. Vickie, do you speak Spanish? Yes. Axel said, Se'que trajiste un vestido de co'ctel? Si, but we are going shopping tomorrow after meeting you all, Raymond and I need to step up our game; your family is very classy, so we want to look our best. Thanks Vickie. Raymond, quiza's deberias llevarla a Dallas Galleria? Will do Axel, thanks for the tip; I hear you're getting a new place of your own, be sure to check out the Oaklawn location, I think you and Daniel will be content living there, it's a great and safe area, I have some gay friends that lives there. Axel asked, Paul you have gay friends that are out of the closet? Paul answered yea, surprised; Don't be, people are the same all over the world. Axel said, really.

Everyone starting to leave, and my mom was seeing everyone to the door, kissing and saying their goodbyes.

(Daniel and Axel stayed and went to the kitchen to put things away and clean up for Ms. Kingston, so she won't have so much to do.)

Daniel said I wish I could stay overnight with you. Axel laughed and said, Daniel, that's not possible, it'll be once we get some of our affairs together, and besides, our parents were nice enough to accept us we don't want to take them too fast. Daniel replied, oh, of course not.

Axel said, I'm going to get a wonderful place for us to move into before we go to College, I look forward to waking up to you every morning, can you imagine waking up to my hard dick every morning, you think you can oversee that? Daniel replied, oh yeah, no problem, I got you bruh.

so, after the party we're going to be very busy, I want us to live as a couple immediately after high school graduation ceremony and the party, I want us to be ready to move into our new place; I'm going to get with the realtor as soon as possible, my dad will assist.

Axel asked, Daniel do you feel like you have a wealthy boyfriend? Daniel said, I still feel the same way I did when I met you. Daniel asked Axel, what about you? Axel answered, I feel like a wealthy and important person. (They're laughing.)

Axel and Jamal's parents, Dr Jay and Jane Allard are working to get their home set up with the caterers. Axel offered to help with the cost of the party, but Dr Jay said, Axel we already have paid for everything, so don't worry we just want you all to have an enjoyable time, because you all deserves it. Jamal talks about you all, we look forward to meeting everyone, especially your parents. Axel replied, thank you Dr Allard.

Jamal went to run some errands while I were at his home working, putting things together with his parents.

Finally, he arrived home and said hello to his parents, he asked, am I in the right home? Yes you are, so you can get busy, there's still things to do. Jamal said, okay dad I need to speak with Axel first; dad don't forget we'll need parking space for our guests, consider it done son.

He asked, Axel will you come with me, I followed him to his room and as soon as I entered the room with him, he said you like my parents. Axel said of course I do, what's up dude, are you okay? Jamal said, dude, I'm very nervous about the graduation ceremony, and the party. tears rolling down Jamal's face; Axel said, come here dude, Axel hugged him and said dude you'll be fine, we all will be with you, Jamal lean forward to kiss Axel, Axel kissed him back, tears continues to roll down Jamal's face, Axel wiped Jamal's face with the palm of his hand, Jamal said, I want us to be as close in college as we are now, Axel replied, of course dude. Jamal, I did something of which you might not approve. Jamal said please do tell? I promised to introduce you to Daniel's brother, he wants to get to know you. Jamal said, no problem, I will love to meet him, what is his name? Paul Bernal, he's 21 years old. Jamal asked, why does he want to meet me? I answered, he kind of into guys. Jamal said, fuck dude, did you tell him about us, I said no Jamal but, I told him you might be interested. Jamal said, okay I'll only do it because you asked. Axel said, great! Also, Jamal, Daniel and I are going to live together, I'm getting us a place in the next few weeks. Jamal said, I respect that, and I won't get in the way because I can clearly see you guys are in love. Axel said, thanks dude, but you remember we are always besties, you'll be in my life forever.

Axel said I have to go; tell your parents I'll see them tomorrow. Okay dude. Axel left, leaving in his new BMW, his hair blowing in the air, waving bye to Jamal and his parents. He thought to himself, I feel like I'm dreaming, my life continues to accelerate, I have a feeling there's much more to come.

Today is the ceremony, everyone got their invitations to the party, and they had some extra, Axel gave them to some of Daniel's cool mates, without Daniel's knowledge. This is the kind of behavior Axel is trying to refrain from.

He has fucked some of Daniel's football mates, one night Peter called Axel at his home and asked him would you like to come over to watch a movie with me, no one's home? Axel asked have you been drinking dude? Peter said no. Okay than you can come and get me, hurry, this is on the low.

They arrived at Peter's home, Peter said Axel no one has to know we are hanging out, I just wanted to see you alone, let's go to my room. Axel followed him and said what are you watching on the TV? Nothing dude, I'm going to get a beer, you want one? Axel said, no thanks dude, But when you get back I'll be naked, Peter said, cool. Peter is Asian, 5"8 150lbs, much heavier than Axel. He came into the room, Axel lying on his bed, with his dick hard, pointed upward. Peter said, damm dude you are fucking sexy! Peter came out of his clothes, is fat, short hard boner pointed toward me; he said, Axel I want to fuck you in your ass? Axel said, no dude, I do the fucking, the most I'll do is give you some head. Peter said, I have never been fucked before; Axel asked, so you have been with other guys. Peter answered yeah dude, But I didn't get fucked. Axel said Peter, here's the deal, I fuck you tonight and I'll owe you one? Peter lied down on his back and Axel had lude, putting it in Peter's ass and finger fucked him until Peter ass hole were soft and loose. Axel said peter, put your legs on my shoulders, he did and said go in slowly Axel.

Axel begin fucking Peter's ass, Peter ass is a lot larger than anyone Axel has ever fucked, Axel asked, dude you like my dick in your ass? Peter only moaned, saying keep fucking me, Axel came out and said turn over, Peter rolled over and Axel went in again, spreading Peter's butt cheeks, going in and out of Peter's ass. Axel said you have the best ass I have ever fucked, (which is what Axel tells everyone,) I'm going to fucking cum now, pounding Peter's ass.

Peter said dude, I am Fucking Cumming, Axel continue pounding and saying, fuck dude I'm Fucking Cumming too, keep throwing your fat ass back on my dick. Peter said bust dude.

When they were done, Axel said, I know I won't hear about this anywhere, standing in front of Peter with his long boner in Peter's face? Peter massaging Axel's dick, he said never, you can trust me. Axel said could I use your bathroom? Peter said, yes and there's a towel in the cabinet, as Axel were walking to the bath Peter watching Axel ass, thinking to himself damm, I wanted to put my tongue in Axel's muscle toned ass.

Peter taken Axel home and they never mentioned it again, so, Daniel doesn't know Axel has a history with some of his mates. Axel's naïveté never meant to hurt Daniel, to Axel it's only a short sexual infatuation, he's for filling; Axel is being self-centered, Daniel will have to do something, or Axel will continue. Axel's attitude, has to stop; he's jeopardizing his relationship with Daniel it may not end well for Axel.

The rules Listed in the invitation noted: That no one can drive from the graduation ceremony to the after party, they would have to have drivers to drop them off and pick them up or it's their parents responsibility. No exceptions: everyone must wear suits and cocktail dresses; each invitation includes one guest. Limited alcohol only serve to 18 year old's and above. All parents are welcomed but is also required to dress semi formal.

CEO's Preparatory High School, Graduating 200 students; Class of 1980: Keynote speaker, Dr Allard, Jamal's dad, Ceremony at the University Park Convention Center, begins at 5pm-8pm, The after party at Jamal's home at 9pm.

Axel's dad made all the arrangements for Axel and Daniel to live in a lakeside resort for a few weeks until they get their home, Axel's dad is purchasing for him; Axel will make sure that happens pronto.

Axel is going to drive them there immediately after the party is over and everyone leaves safely. Paul gave Axel some overnight things in a backpack for Daniel; Axel has things for himself in his trunk. Daniel doesn't know about the lakeside resort, where he and Axel will stay until they find a place of their own.

Everyone punctually arrived at the ceremony, it was a beautiful site to see, the graduation robes are, dark blue and gold. The parents sitting in the audience with total excitement in their eyes, as the students crossed the stage to receive their diplomas, the parents applauding. The ceremony went exceedingly well.

People started to arrive at Jamal's home; Jamal, Daniel and Axel with Jamal's parents at the door greeting people as they arrived. Katy, her mom, and a guy no one were familiar with, he's Katie's new boyfriend, they were some of the first to arrive. Daniel said hello Katy, she respond, hello everyone, this is my mother Mrs. Wilson, this is my boyfriend Zachary. Everyone said hello, Katy said to Daniel, Daniel maybe we can have the talk tonight? Daniel replied, yes, maybe.

Daniel said nice to meet you Zachary, Katy has mentioned you to me before. Zachary replied, I've heard a lot about you, I'm sure we'll get to know each other's soon; Daniel respond, for sure dude, nice to meet you, maybe we will talk later? I would be happy to know what you do, and where you're from. Zachary respond, yes Daniel, just pull my coat tail, I'm happy to be here and to meet you all.

The Coach and his boyfriend came, Axel was very happy to introduce him to everyone, Daniel were happy to see him, and happy Axel is still participating in the group.

Paul arrived with his parents; Paul wearing a dark gray suit with a dark blue bow tie, looking very successful, Mr. and Ms. Banal, look exquisite, Axel is wearing a navy blue pin stripe suit with a dotted bow tie, they all look very professional; As soon as they walked in Paul immediately went to Axel and hugged him, saying you cleaned up well; said hello to everyone, Axel said, Paul this is Jamal and his parents. Paul said hello everyone thanks for the invitation, I'm very happy to meet you all; I'm Daniel's older brother. They all said their hello's.

Jamal was immediately interested in Paul, he said Paul let's get a drink. Paul said, oh, okay, I'll follow you, they shook hand, and walked toward the bar.

Axel's family arrived in a family limousine, Axel's dad didn't won't anyone driving; Mr. Kingston doesn't drink anymore, but the rest of the family does; Mr. Kingston is totally against drunk driving; Mrs. Kingston accompanied by her boyfriend, James, they all road together, dressed for success. Mrs. Kingston said to Axel, I'll come find you we're going to have a chat; have an enjoyable time son. Mr. Kingston said hello Daniel you look very handsome. Daniel respond, Gracias señor, usted también se ve guapo; Daniel wearing a dinner jacket with sequence. Axel replied, okay mom is everything okay? Yes son, no worries.

Everyone greets one another with kisses and hugs, saying it's so nice to meet you. All of the parents met in the Doctor's designated room, that's set up with everything they will need totally comfortable, with a personal waiter. Everyone hits it off and the party begins.

Axel convinced Dr. Allard to let him be responsible for the music and entertainment, Axel paid 10 thousand dollars. Raymond and his traveling companion will perform, they're going to sing two sets, one of the duets titled, "You're All I Need To Get By." Raymond gather a group of musicians, for live music, and a DJ stand setup on the back lawn, there will also be a one hour comedy skit, there's four actors, their all handsome Latino men. Raymond made all the contacts for Axel to hire.

During the party, Axel dad took out time to speak with Axel alone at a table on the back lawn. He said, Axel I see you're a poplar man around here, well respected; Impressive. I know you can take care of yourself and Daniel, perhaps you and Daniel should keep a lower profile just for safety, especially when you guys move into your own place, you can't be so trusting with other people, everyone doesn't have your best interest at heart, so maybe you should keep your circle of friends small like we talked about. Daniel already stands out like a wealthy, accomplished man. Thanks dad I love him, he's beautiful to me.

I won't you to consult with me, or our wealth manager advisor before you make any large purchases; your trust fund account will not be released to you until after two years of you graduating from college, and even than you'll have a financial advisor, it's for your protection, and we have a family lawyer as well, you'll meet in the next few days, you'll be contacted as soon as you get the time, please make it sooner than later. Axel replied, yes sir, you're right, I'll need a lot of help, and Daniel is my partner and he's completely loyal to me.

I don't know the role Daniel plays in your life, but I see you must love him, and I like him as well. What do you think about me paying his College intuition to help him out? Dad, Daniel's family does well, I like the idea, but Daniel doesn't need any help, I'll have to speak with him first. Axel's dad said I'm going to start a business here in Dallas and Atlanta, Liz and I will have a home in both cities, it's a business decision, I have plans for us to increase our wealth.

This is what we'll working on while you guys are completing college, we are going to create a family dynasty.

Mr. Kingston said, are you okay with the lakeside resort? Axel said, it's great! do we own the place? Yes son, think of it as an investment. Dad we are planning to stay there only until I find us a home, in Dallas. Mr. Kingston asked, Son please explain to me how it works being with a man, are you the head of the relationship? Yes sir, but I don't make decisions about our lives alone, (Daniel understands I make the final decisions about our lives and everything else.) Mr. Kingston said, that's my son, (you're just like your dad.)

Axel I know you and your brother are close but, don't be concern about your brother, he get the same financial assist, and advisor as you, to help managing his money, I love him and he's trust worthy. One other thing, we need a grandson for your father? Well dad, I will have to work on that, I read something about artificial insemination by accident, I were intrigued by it, it'll require a female to engage, maybe someday dad there's no rush; I think I'll live long enough to make that decision, or maybe I'll get Daniel pregnant; They laughed for a second then, Mr. Kingston said don't be silly son. Axel dad said, okay Axel, let's go mingle, I like meeting new people. They hugged and went separate direction. Axel said, good talk dad, you have an enjoyable night.

Axel mom walked up, She said to Axel's dad don't leave because I came. No Joann, we were done talking, you need me? No, I just wanted to have a word with Axel. Okay, he's all yours. Let's sit down Axel; They sat down, Mrs. Kingston asked, how are you son? I'm good mom, she said you look very handsome. Thanks mom, I don't think I have ever seen you look so beautiful. Thanks son.

I wanted talk to you about what my plans are, James and I are buying a home in New Hampshire, and we plan to open a small business; we're going to live there, we will return for your graduation from college in four years. I know we have never been apart, but you're a young man now, I know you'll be fine here in Dallas, with Daniel. What do you think? Mom, all this has been overwhelming, but I'm okay, I have a lot to get used to and I look forward to the changes in our lives. Mom, what about your home here? I need you to keep the upkeep on the house, we will decide later what we're going to do with it. Your dad will be closest to you and he's going to make sure everything goes well for you here in Dallas, if you're not okay with all the changes I don't really have to leave, I just wanted to do somethings I have always wanted to do. No mom, I'll be fine, and I'll call you to keep you updated, I want you to be happy, you trust Mr. James? Yes, he's a good man and I want to be with him. We are a couple, he has family there, their expecting us; I'm going to make all the arrangements; James and I are going to leave next week. No worries mom. I'll call you probably every day until we're all settle. Yes mom I expect you will.

Great son, we'll talk more, you have fun with your friends, oh by the way, you all did an awesome job putting all this together. Thanks mom, I love you. Thanks Axel.

Axel mentioned to Daniel at the party some of what he and his dad talked about. Daniel told Axel, you and your dad can't buy me, you are being controlling, I love you no matter what and I don't need your money. Axel respond, Daniel don't get upset my job is to take care of you, we'll talk more about this later; Axel if you meant you'll take care of me financially, no thanks, I can take care of myself. Axel respond, Daniel this is a party will you please, calm down, and don't speak so loudly, someone could hear you; it's not a good look for us. Also, my mom is moving to New Hampshire, she said she'll return in four years, after we completed college. Wow, really? Yes, so it looks like it's just us. Axel don't worry, I'm your partner and I will always be here with. Thanks Daniel it's going to be wonderful.

Daniel I have some surprises for you after the party; Daniel asked, where will we stay tonight? Axel replied, you are going to stay with me for the rest of your life, (without any exception,) I'll oversee that, you just ride the waves. Be sure to spend some time with Katy, we might need to put her on our payroll, Oh yeah, check on your mates to see if there's something they need; Daniel said, Axel you don't need to worry about my mates I'll take care of them. Axel said, of course you will; I'm going to be an attorney and I need to know as many people as possible for the business, they are potential clients, I need to mingle, Axel shook and kissed Daniel's hand and said, (You Are My Prince). Daniel said, you think you're my king? Axel replied, yes and I'll prove it to you tonight, he pulled Daniel into his arms, whispered in Daniel's ear, you're the most handsome man here, I feel privileged to be the guy that takes you home tonight. Axel kissed Daniel and said I'll see you at the end of the party.

Katy saw Daniel standing at the bar alone, she walked up behind him and pinched his ass, and said hello handsome, you're drinking now? Hi Katy, you look beautiful; No, I'm not but tonight after the party I'm going to have a drink with Axel privately, are you and Zachary drinking? she answered, just wine and Zachary is out back with the guys smoking a joint. Daniel asked, you're okay with him smoking cannabis? Yes, it's no big deal, we do it at his apartment sometimes. Daniel said tell Zachary I want to take one with me when this is over, Axel and I will smoke it tonight when we're alone. Daniel went on asking Katy, are you going to live with? No, I'm going to live on campus. Katy asked, can we talk about you and Axel now?

Daniel said, why not; Katy, Axel is my boyfriend and we're going to live together while in college. Really! I knew you were in love with Axel. So, you're gay? YES. Katy asked so what was that with me? Daniel respond, I wasn't sure about what I wanted. She said and you are now? Yes, very sure. Axel in love with? Yes, but sometimes I'm not so sure, he's very controlling, I feel he thinks I'm a trophy. That's funny Daniel. Is that Axel's BMW I see him driving sometimes? Daniel said yes, he's a very wealthy man now, he paid $10,000 for the entertainment tonight, thanks to his (daddy,) but we have to talk about that later.

Axel has changed my life, a life I'm not too comfortable with. Why is that Daniel? Axel's dad is a millionaire and he's spoiling Axel rotten, and Axel is in a sexuality group, because he has a problem with controlling himself, he's been unfaithful to me. Really, with guys at our school? YES. She said,

Daniel you stand your ground, maybe you should live on campus with me? No that would break his heart. I don't want to lose him; my parents think I should wait until I'm totally sure I want to be with. Katy asked, your parents are aware of your sexual preference? Yes, I told them and their okay with. Katy said, Wow, SMU just got more interesting.

Katy, Axel likes you; he want us all to be close friends so, be cool with and try not to let him know, you are aware he's a millionaire, his dad told him to keep it on the low; and that'll upset him if he think I've told others. I understand Daniel, I love you and we'll always be besties. Thank you Katy, and I love you as well. I think I'll have a drink for the first time, join me girlfriend? Now you're talking Daniel. Katy said, let's toast to the rich and your first love journey. (Their laughing)

Daniel's brother Paul is spending a lot of time with Jamal, it seems to be going great for them; Paul said to Jamal, it looks like you're going to need help cleaning up after the party? Jamal answered, no dude the help is going to take care of everything.

Jamal said, It's 9 pm, the party will ends shortly after midnight, the help will be here until after everything is cleaned up; my parents is going to help seeing everyone off, they're going to bed soon after that. Their Doctor's, they always leave at 5am, heading to the hospital they work the first shift hours.

Paul asked, it sounds like you are asking me to sleep over with you tonight, are you gay? Jamal answered, no dude do I have to be? Paul said, fuck no dude. Jamal asked, are you gay, if so I'm cool with? Paul asked, you want me to sleep on your floor? Jamal said, no we'll sleep in the same bed, are you afraid? Jamal said don't answer that; How about we get a beer and go out back with the guys to get a couple of hits, we're sort things out later.

Paul said okay Jamal, looking Jamal in his eyes trying to make sure Jamal is coming on to him, before he makes his move in response, Paul has a hard on, he said, Jamal I'll meet you outside, my big dick is throbbing; I have to pee, please excuse me. Jamal said I can't help you with that, see you outside dude and don't get lost. Paul thinking to himself, yeah, Jamal wants to fuck.

The party has end, our guest are leaving, Jamal and Paul are tipsy, still hanging closely, looking like a couple. Daniel, and Axel is at the door seeing everyone off. Axel, wanted to make sure no one is driving. Axel looked out the door, there were a line of limousines, parents in their cars waiting and taxi cabs lined up as well. All the families are leaving, their very happy to see everything went well, Axel's dad said to Axel, son please don't stay out too late, when are you going to leave? Axel answered in about an hour, just wanted to make sure everything is wrapped up. Mr. Kingston asked, have you had any drinks are smoked weed tonight? No dad, I'm totally sober, but thanks for asking.

Raymond and Vickie heading to the airport to catch their flight, Axel said bruh I love you please call me as soon as you get where you and Vickie are going, thanks for helping me with the entertainment, the song you and Vickie sang was very touching. Raymond, please be careful, with tears in their eyes, they are hugging, I'm going to miss you. He kissed Axel and said peace out bruh.

Zachery and Katy are leaving out the door, Axel kissed Katy and said, thanks for coming; Zachery said, Axel we didn't get a chance to chat, you and Daniel has an open visitation to visit me at my apartment. Axel and Daniel said thanks dude, we'll see you and Katy very soon. By the way Zachery, what do you do for a living? He answered, for now I'm in the US Navy. Oh, cool, we will talk soon,

Daniel and I are getting settled in our new home, but we'll get with you before we go back to school.

Everyone is gone, Daniel and Axel are leaving; Axel said, Daniel you can leave your jeep, I'm going to drive us. Daniel said I'm excited to see where you're taking me. Daniel has a joint and Axel has a bottle of champagne, Don Pérignon, they're going to get stone once their at their new home for now; this wasn't planned, they're surprising one another.

Daniel said, Axel it was good to see everyone, one of our guests brought an old friend, his name is Bryce, we were good friends. Axel asked, were? Daniel replied, yes, he and his family moved to Plano, Tx; Axel said, remember the trajectory is to keep our circle small, are you planning to hang with? our future is much larger than just one old friend, Axel went on saying; I guess I'm cool with, if you must. Daniel said, Great! don't over think it you have nothing to be jealous about, I want you to meet him. Axel replied, I'll probably be too busy, you can set it up later. Are you cool with that Daniel? Sounds good Axel.

Axel and arrived at the resort, they drove 20 minutes north of Dallas to Richmond Hills; Axel were there once with Raymond and their dad to show Axel around, and some of the house functions; Axel still feels amazingly surprised.

Daniel said, Axel what the fuck, are you joking dude. No Daniel this is your new home. Axel used a code to open the gate, as they drove a half mile from the gate, lights lit up outside the driveway as he drove to the four car garage. Daniel eyes wide open, he's holding Axel by his thigh. He said, Axel this place is huge, I don't know if I can do this, could we stay somewhere else? No Daniel this is our home for now, take a deep breath and when you're ready we'll go in, keep in mind It's only for now. My dad bought the place as an investment, it's a vacation resort.

Daniel said, I'm ready Axel let's go in, do you have a key? No, I have the code, there are keys but they're in an access box, that also requires the same code. I'll show you later. Daniel walked in behind Axel and said, WOW! How many rooms are there? Axel answered, six bedrooms and one master Bedroom, there is a small pond behind the house. Axel said, wait stand here I have to go to the car and get some things. Daniel stood in the exact spot, until Axel returned. Daniel asked, is that my backpack? Axel said, yeah, I picked up some of your things and I'm wearing your bowtie I'm surprised you didn't notice; Daniel said I did notice, I were wondering when did you get it. Paul gave it to me for good luck.

Axel we have a phone number? Yes, I'll give it to you later. We'll go to get more of your things later this week when you're ready; I have another surprise for you, but Let's look around first. Daniel reached out for Axel to hold his hand, Axel asked, you're okay? Let's go up to our master bedroom, we can get comfortable. This place is totally furnished and well supplied, we have everything we need, it's like a dream. They stood in the foyer, Axel kissing Daniel's neck slowly unbutton his shirt, holding him close whispering in his ear, you are my man and I love you, still kissing him massaging his chest moving his hand down Daniel's pants. Daniel holding his head back, moaning. Axel asked, put your tongue in my mouth, with his hand in Daniel's pants. Daniel said, Axel let's go to our room.

Once they were in the room, Daniel said, this is amazing, Axel how will we live here? Axel answered, comfortably. This is a resort for rich families, my dad only bought the place for cash flow, you will learn about that later in college.

Daniel said, let's take our clothes off, and lie in bed together, would you mind if we didn't make love tonight? Axel asked, what about your surprise I have for you? Daniel said, okay, what do you have for me? Axel said, I have one bottle of the best champagne that money can buy; Daniel replied, really, I guess great minds think alike; I have a joint. Axel said yea, I don't smoke weed, I'll only do it with you just this once. Daniel asked, where is it, Axel said, I'll go down stairs and get it, it's in the refrigerator with two chilled glasses, you get undressed and will go out on the master balcony to smoke, there's matching robe's in that closet over there, Axel pointed at the double doors, and Daniel if you don't want to have sex tonight it's okay with me we can just love on each other without having sex; your kiss taste like alcohol have you been drinking? Si, I had two drinks with Katy; Daniel said, I just need to process everything that has happened. Hurry back I have more surprises for you.

Axel returned with the Champagne and glasses, Daniel lying on the bedroom sofa with his robe open. Axel said, fuck dude, you're so fucking sexy, I'm a rich man with a sexy boyfriend, handing a drink to Daniel, Daniel replied, thanks Axel.

Daniel said, Axel I have two gold rings, each one is with our name engraved; will you wear one with me to express our feelings we have for each other, this is for us to be identified as a couple? If I had known we were going to be rich I would have spent more for them. Axel said yes I'm honored, I love the rings they are beautiful, I have a surprise for you as well. Tomorrow I'll meet with my attorney, I'm going to deposit $500,000 In your bank account, I'm not being controlling but I want you to have your own funds so that when you want, you can buy whatever you need, think of it as a fresh start from me, you should be as independent has I am; and maybe you will hire a decorator to decorate our new home and the office, before we move in. Please accept my gift to you, I love you and in my heart you are my spouse. Axel getting undressed, putting his robe on; Daniel said, yes Axel I'll accept the money, I'm truly thankful, you are a wonderful man!

Daniel said, Axel come sit next to me. Daniel begin kissing Axel, running his fingers through Axel's hair, saying I have to learn how to love you all over again as your spouse, I'll be better than the others, I'll be the best man you ever had; loyal and faithful. You must be faithful to me, do whatever you need to do but don't fuck up, you need to be committed to our relationship; If my love for you doesn't bring you home that means I'm not enough for you, but yes, I'll ask my mom to decorate our new locations, and I'll give her a substantial donation for her charities. By the way Axel, I love your after five beard, maybe you should keep it for me. Axel said, I'll do whatever you want me to do. Daniel, now that we know that we tested negative for all sexual diseases, including HIV; You think we could have sex without condoms now? Maybe, I don't think you're ready for that, let's not rush it. Whatever you think Daniel, I'm in love with you, but it's all up to you when you're ready.

(This is a whole new life for them, and it has just begun.)

To be continue

- Epilogue

Axel and Daniel are convinced their Soulmates, and nothing will change that; they can't seem to keep their relationship free from infidelity, if Daniel knew all the guys that Axel have told, "Daniel can't ever know what we did;" There's a chance he could leave Axel.

Axel has a misconception of, "free to be myself," He has taken the phrase to a hold nother level. Axel's family as always treated Axel like he is special which has caused Axel to be self-serving, if anyone is disloyal it's Axel but he doesn't see it that way, he's going to blame everyone but himself for the things he has done secretly with other guys. Including with Paul. The good thing is for the sake of his relationship with Daniel, he's going to continue attending the gay group, it's a place for him to admit his short comings and seek the will to change. Daniel no longer attends the group; he didn't think there was need for him to attend.

Axel and Daniel's parents wasn't surprised when they came out as gay men, they felt the inevitable was somehow obvious. The only explanation they have is, sexual assignment is at birth. Axel mom, Ms. Kingston said she or their dad never talked with their sons about sex, "my sons embraced their sexuality willingly. I also know my sons has never been pressured into doing something they weren't comfortable with, "my sons embraced nature's will."

Axel will find out two can play the same game as him; Daniel will be approached by a college mate, what he's offering to Daniel, Daniel will highly consider the offer. Daniel is raised to be a smart and honest man, not a push over, people that know Daniel have a lot of respect for him he has a strong personality, and he certainly can take care of himself, his only weakness is Axel and the love he has for him; he feels he is responsible for Axel because he was Axel's first time with a man sexually.

"Axel and Daniel, first love Journey", is the beginning of two young bilingual high schoolers, which met and felt instant chemistry that leads to a love affair. Daniel would be petrified to find out there's a lot about Axel he never knew, if he did it could lead to ultimately devastation to their relationship.

Axel finds himself in awkward situations with guys and he gives in to them every time, Axel feels he is still coming into himself and finds it hard to refuse a chance to fuck a guy that says, "I'm not gay Axel," Axel like being the first.

Let's be clear, Axel always have sex wearing a condom. No exceptions.

Their relationship will continue running into obstacles, but their future will go on and will become extraordinary, they will have to learn to live a life they could have never imagined.

Meanwhile, they will enjoy being in college and become very successful and that's one of the components that holds them together. Their parents will always be in their lives, they all will become one big family.

Axel's dad returned back to Dallas, Texas and changed their lives completely, given them a whole new life to live.

All of Axel and Daniel's friends will continue to be bestie with them, Paul and Axel will become closer friends, which could be described as too close. Paul will be there at every turn of Axel's life, even though he and Jamal is in an open relationship; Paul didn't feel the need to tell anyone he's bisexual.

To be clear; Having a clear understanding about who you are, will require us to love ourselves; we must live a respectful life as everyone else.

We are responsible for our own actions; life is more enjoyable when we be honest with ourselves and those that are around us, same sex relationships are no different; So, embrace whom you are.

I was inspired while drafting this book, I hope my readers are just as inspired while reading, Axel and Daniels, First Love Journey. This taken place when Cellular Phones wasn't available to the general population, this is during the mid-70's. The continuation of the upcoming storyline will begin in 1986, Technology is much different, with cellular phones, a more modern system.

- Acknowledgement:

I would like to extend my deepest thanks to the LGBTQ community around the world. Also, people that's bilingual I hope my Spanish is acceptable.

My people that are in hiding I hope I reached you all from my book, it's my desire for you to find the strength to come out of the closet, but you are not alone, it's understandable if you think is too difficult, but sometimes the hardest part is having confidence in ourselves; for me that's where I started, accepting who I am.

Special thanks to libraries around the world that's on the front line fighting to keep our book of all kinds in our library's. Thanks to erotic bookstores, also all the outlets that make our books available to the public.

Special thanks to family members and my son VanDawn Isadore, thanks son for coming out to me and the family; I truly thank you all for your love and support. (This book is my dedication to you).

At last, but not at all least; Thanks to my readers for taking the time to read my book, you purchased my book with your money, and I am utterly thankful. There will be book two and three that will come out in year 2023, I hope you are inspired to purchase the next two books.

My fictional, love erotic story came from two young men that came out and found peace and joy.

These two men will go on to live full lives within the society as we know it to be, there's room at the table for everyone.

Speaking metaphorically, Axel and Daniel, the rest of their circle is in every community around the world; they're representations of ordinary people.

I hope you all enjoyed reading this eBook; I hope to hear from you after reading my beloved project. Please post your reviews or emails me with any thoughts or concerns. Book two and three will be available in year 2023. Thanks so much.

Made in the USA
Middletown, DE
17 November 2022